FR

'Frankie,' said this is Frankie, who's going to be your new sister.'

Jasper and Frankie glanced furtively at each other then quickly looked away again. I don't want to be anyone's sister, thought Frankie. Maybe Jasper didn't want to be anyone's brother. His eyes were all red and watery. He looked as if he had been crying; or as if he were about to cry.

'Isn't this nice?' beamed Frankie's mum. 'All the family gathered round?'

'Smashing,' said Billy. 'And afterwards –' He winked at Frankie's mum. 'Who knows?'

Frankie's mum giggled. Frankie looked at her, crossly. She hated people giggling when she didn't know what they were giggling about.

Also available in Beaver by Jean Ure

YOU TWO
A BOTTLED CHERRY ANGEL

FRANKIE'S DAD

Jean Ure

Beaver Books

To my friend, Emma Chandler

A Beaver Book
Published by Arrow Books Limited
62-65 Chandos Place, London WC2N 4NW

An imprint of Century Hutchinson Limited

London Melbourne Sydney Auckland
Johannesburg and agencies throughout
the world

First published in 1988 by Hutchinson Children's Books
Beaver edition 1989

Set in Garamond by BookEns, Saffron Walden, Essex

Printed and bound in Great Britain by
Courier International Ltd, Tiptree, Essex

ISBN 0 09 959720 9

1

Frankie Foster was up a tree. The rest of them – Hake-face Heneghan, Terence Townell, and Ghulam Ahmed (more usually known as the Toenail and the Gool) – were clustered on the ground looking up.

'Betcha daren't jump!' yelled Hake-face.

'Bet I do!' yelled Frankie.

'Betcha don't!'

'Bet I do!'

'Betcha don't!'

'Bet I do!'

'Go on, then, do it!'

There was a pause, as Frankie silently measured the distance between up here and down there. It was certainly a long way.

'I wouldn't,' said the Gool.

'No,' jeered Hake-face. 'I bet I know someone else as wouldn't, neither!'

That was a challenge. It was more than a challenge: it was an insult.

'Get out the way!' screeched Frankie. 'I'm coming down!'

They scattered, just in time. THUD! went Frankie, hitting the ground.

'Stupid git,' said Hake-face. He turned, contemptuously, to show how unimpressed he was. So Frankie Foster had jumped out of a tree! So what? Jumping out of trees was no big deal. Anybody could do it if they set their minds to

5

it. If they had to. Like if there was a fire or something. No point risking death just for the sake of it, was there? 'Stupid thing to do!'

The uncomfortable fact remained, however, that Frankie had done it and that Hake had not. Frankie Foster was always doing things that other people couldn't quite screw up the courage to do. Really crazy, dangerous things they were sometimes, like running across the railway line and tightrope walking on the parapet above the canal: things that made your blood run cold.

'Race you to the fountain!' shrieked Hake-face, setting off at a gallop before Frankie even had a chance to get up. It was the only way he could think of to restore confidence. He could beat the other two easily enough, but Frankie Foster could run as fast as any boy. Lots of people thought she *was* a boy. Hake had at first; their first day at Juniors. Well, it wasn't surprising, the way she lopped her hair and went round all butch and bellicose in her boiler suit, bashing people.

Hake took off in the direction of the fountain, Toenail and the Gool hot on his heels. Frankie, furious, leapt to her feet and tore after them, flying like the wind over the rough springy grass of the Heath. She could beat that Hake-face any day of the week – except when he cheated. 'Pig!' she shrieked, arriving at the fountain only seconds behind the rest of them. 'Cheaty rotten pig!'

'What's your problem?' Hake stuck his fingers in her face. 'Just 'cos you come last!'

Frankie hurled herself on him, fists a-flail. Toenail, who came from a Good Family and was only allowed to mix with the likes of Frankie Foster and Hake-face Heneghan as long as he didn't get into any fights, stood watching from a safe distance, along with the Gool who lacked the aggressive instinct.

'What's the time, anyway?' panted Frankie, as the fight

6

came to an amicable end, one black eye for one cut lip.

'Twenny to four,' said Toenail.

'Twenny to four? I gotta get back! My mum'll flay me!'

'*In*doors, *in* bath, by three o'clock sharp!' That was what her mother had said. Mopping at her cut lip with the edge of her T-shirt, Frankie turned and began to trot back across the Heath. The others trotted with her. They didn't have to be indoors and in the bath by three o'clock sharp, but where Frankie went they tended to follow.

'Why you gotta be in so early?' the Gool wanted to know.

Frankie pulled a hideous face. '*He's* coming.'

'What, your mum's bloke?'

'Yeah.' She pulled an even worse face – her mum's bloke, that she was getting married to.

'What's his name?'

'Billy Small.' Frankie put all the scorn and loathing that she could into it.

Hake-face guffawed and did a little caper in the air. 'Billy Small's only got one ball, soon he won't have none at all!'

Toenail and the Gool also guffawed and did little capers. They chanted it, happily: 'Billy Small's only got one ball—'

'What you on about?' said Frankie, angrily. She didn't like it when people made jokes that she couldn't understand.

'You wouldn't know, you're only a girl,' jeered Hake.

Frankie stopped, 'You looking for trouble?'

Quickly, before they could start another fight, the Gool said: 'What's he like, then? This geezer?'

'Horrible,' said Frankie. 'I hate him.'

'My mum,' said Toenail, 'says that kids always resent it

when their mums get married; when they get married a second time, that is. She says it's only to be expected, just at the beginning, till you get used to it.'

Oh! So Toenail's mum said that, did she? Frankie tossed her head. Fat lot Mrs Clever Clogs Toenail knew about it! For her information, Frankie didn't resent Billie Small, she despised him and loathed him; and anyway, Frankie's mum could hardly be getting married for a second time considering she'd hadn't even been married for a first time, so just put that in your pipe and smoke it, Mrs Clever Clogs!

'My mum,' said Toenail, 'says it's only natural you should feel a bit jealous.'

'Me?' screeched Frankie. '*Jealous*?'

'Only a bit.' Toenail took a hasty step backwards. 'But it's perfectly natural. That's what my mum says.'

'Your mum talks a load of crap! I'm not jealous! Jealous of that creep? Nasty fat thing like a piggy-eyed elephant?'

'I like elephants,' said the Gool.

'You wouldn't if your mum was going to marry one! I wouldn't *mind*,' said Frankie, 'if she was marrying someone nice – someone like Mr Harding. Be all right if she married Mr Harding.'

Hake-face scoffed. 'How can she marry Mr Harding when he's s'posed to be your granddad?'

Frankie felt her cheeks grow hot. It wasn't the first time she had been caught out by her own inventions. She'd forgotten she'd told them about Mr Harding being her grandfather. He wasn't, of course; he was her mother's employer. He owned the big house where they lived and where Frankie's mum was the housekeeper.

'I didn't mean that Mr Harding,' said Frankie, 'I meant another Mr Harding.'

'Oh, yeah?'

'Yeah!'

'Pull the other one,' said Hake, scornfully. 'Your mum

don't know any other Mr Hardings! Anyway, you're a double-dyed liar, Frankie Foster – Mr Harding ain't your granddad.'

'How d'you know?' demanded Frankie, belligerently.

Hake tapped the side of his nose. 'I know 'cos I know!'

'*How* d'you know?'

''Cos I do!'

'You don't know nothing, Hake Heneghan!'

'I know a sight more'n you do!'

The argument continued right the way across the Heath. It continued down Heath Street, and on into the High Street, and up the hill to Beechcroft Road, and on as far as number twelve, which was Mr Harding's house where Frankie's mum did the housekeeping. There they parted company.

'See ya,' said Frankie.

'See ya,' said Hake.

No one bore any grudges; they all knew that Frankie Foster was the most terrible liar, just as they all knew that Hake stole things and that Toenail had a loopy sister and that the Gool wet the bed. (They knew about the Gool wetting the bed because he had done it last year at summer camp.) They all knew everything there was to know about one another, and they all knew that they all knew, which meant that nobody could snitch. Frankie wasn't ever going to find any friends like Hake and the Gool and Toenail. Certainly she wasn't going to find any in a place like Worple Park.

Worple Park! Who but a piggy-eyed creep like Billie Small would live in a place called Worple Park? Frankie had looked it up on the tube map. It was miles away from Hampstead – thirteen stops, no less. She had counted them. First you had to get the tube to King's Cross, on the black line, which was the Northern; then another tube, on the Piccadilly, the blue bobbly one, all the way out to

9

Worple Manor; then a bus from Worple Manor. It would take hours and hours and be hideously expensive. She would never be able to come back and play with the gang. They would forget all about her and very soon they wouldn't care.

Why couldn't her mother marry Mr Harding? It would be lovely if she could marry Mr Harding. Then they could stay in Beechcroft Road, and Frankie could go on going to the same school and having the same friends and—

'Frankie Foster, you come indoors this instant!'

That was Frankie's mum; bawling up the basement steps, in a right old rage. Frankie rolled her eyes: *that* would mean a bashing.

'I thought—' biff! – 'I told you—' boff! – 'to be back—' thwack! – 'by three o'clock sharp?'

Frankie shook her head, waiting for the stars to clear. 'I forgot.'

'Did you, now? Isn't that surprising? She forgot! Selfish little devil that you are!' Frankie ducked. 'Never mind that your mother's gettin' married and her boyfriend's comin' round to tea and she wants to make a good impression! Oh, no! That's not important!' Her mother mimicked her. '*I forgot!*'

'It wasn't so much that I forgot, exactly.' Frankie rubbed at her ear, surprised to find it still attached to her head. 'I haven't got a watch.'

'And there aren't any clocks around? And what about that posh friend of yours? Are you telling me he hasn't a watch, either?'

'It's broken,' lied Frankie.

'Oh, yes! I'm sure! And who broke it, I'd like to know? You, probably! You get in there . . .' Frankie's mum took hold of her by her battered ear and jerked her across the basement kitchen towards the poky bathroom with its old Victorian bath (deep-sided with claw feet) and flowered Victorian washbasin. 'You get and scrub yourself, and be

10

quick about it! They'll be here in fifteen minutes and I want you presentable.'

Frankie squirmed, doing her best to wriggle out of her mother's grasp. Frankie's mum was small, and she was thin, but she couldn't half pinch. She had a grip like a pair of pliers.

'Who's they?'

'What do you mean, "Who's they?" You just get those clothes off! All of them! Look at the state of you!'

'They,' said Frankie, 'you said "*they*".' A horrid thought struck her: 'Olive isn't coming, is she?'

Olive was her mum's best mate. Frankie didn't like her. Once a week Olive and Frankie's mum went out together (going on the razzle, Olive called it) and whenever Frankie's mum got back from being out with Olive she was all loud and giggly and stupid. Sometimes she woke Frankie up by crashing about the bedroom, bumping into things and falling over, and once she had gone to sleep with a cigarette in her hand and set light to the bedclothes. She had made Frankie swear not to tell Mr Harding.

It was all Olive's fault. It had to be. It only ever happened when she went out with Olive. And it was Olive who had introduced her to Billie Small; that was another black mark against her. Another reason Frankie couldn't stand her. If Olive were coming—

''Tisn't Olive, it's Billie's little boy.'

Frankie scowled fiercely at her reflection in the bathroom mirror. That was even *worse*. Billie's little boy was only seven years old. Seven-year olds were the dead end. They were *muck*.

'What's he want to go bringing him for?'

'And why shouldn't he bring him? I'm going to be his new mother, aren't I? You're going to be his new sister. Isn't it only natural we should all get to know each other?'

Frankie's scowl deepened. She didn't want to know

11

some mucky seven-year old. 'What's his name, anyway?'

'Jasper.'

'*Jasper?*'

'There's nothing wrong with the name Jasper! It's a perfectly good name. Don't you go startin' any of your nonsense, my girl! I want you to behave yourself for once. Behave like a civilized human being. Just remember this is a poor little chap who's had to be living in a foster home for the past year. A poor little chap without any mother. Try thinking of someone else for a change, instead of yourself – and just get a move on!' Frankie's mum snatched impatiently at Frankie's discarded clothes. 'You get and wash yourself while I fetch some clean things – and mind you do the job thoroughly!'

Frankie, left standing in the bathroom in only her knickers, reached out grumpily for the flannel and soap. Jasper Small, Worple Park . . . this whole thing was crazy. She didn't want to be somebody's new sister! She didn't want to go and live in Worple Park! All very well saying think of someone else, but who ever bothered thinking of her? Her mother obviously didn't or she wouldn't be marrying this piggy-eyed creep; a piggy-eyed creep who worked in a nut house. Just pity the poor nuts! Imagine being a nut with that in charge of you.

Frankie's mum came back into the bathroom carrying a pair of sandals, a pair of white socks, and a little red dress with lace collar and cuffs. Frankie stared, in disbelief. 'What's them?'

'New clothes; I bought them specially for you. Just hurry along, now, and get yourself into them! They'll be here any minute, and—'

'I'm not wearing *that*!' Frankie never wore girls' clothes, except when she absolutely had to, like for school. She certainly wasn't wearing a little red dress with lace on it.

'You'll wear what you're told to wear, young woman!

12

I'm sick of you going round like some scragamuffin! I'm going to have you decent just for once.' Frankie's mum shook out the dress and advanced threateningly upon Frankie. 'Come along, now! On with it!'

Frankie gritted her teeth. 'I'd sooner wear a sack!'

'Do I have to force you?' said her mother.

'Try it!' hissed Frankie.

Her mother raised her arm, hand open for a slap. Seizing the opportunity, Frankie swerved, dived out through the bathroom door and scampered up the passage in her knickers and bare feet; on into the bedroom which she shared with her mother. Her mother chased after her, screaming. 'Any more trouble from you, I'll knock your ruddy head off! So help me, I will! I've had just about as much as I can take ... I'm giving you due warning ... Frankie Foster, will you open that door!'

Frankie held on to the door knob on her side, her mother held on to it on hers. At first Frankie had the advantage because she was holding with both hands while her mother was only holding with one, on account of the red dress; but after a bit the dress was obviously left to take care of itself, for the door knob began to twist quite violently. It twisted and turned and leaped in Frankie's hands like a live thing. Frankie hung on grimly, while at the same time setting her shoulder to the door and pushing against it with all her might. On the other side, her mother was doing exactly the same in the opposite direction, shrieking as she did so.

'I wish to God that I'd put you into a home! I didn't have to keep you, you know ... I could have had you adopted, I had offers enough. I could've got rid of you ten times over! I could have been back in Ireland by now. I could've gone home and nobody any the wiser. God help me, poor fool that I am! I struggle and strive and what thanks do I get? None! Nothing but insolence and ingratitude! I've a good mind to have you put into care! Tell them to come and take you away! You needn't think I'd miss you. Frankie Foster, if you don't open this door I'll murder you, I will!'

'Open it yourself!' screamed Frankie, letting go of the handle. The door crashed open and Frankie's mum fell in.

'You little. . . .'

Frankie, in her knickers, sat cross-legged on the end of the bed, listening to the names her mother was calling her. Most of them she had heard before, but one or two were new. She stored them up in her mind for future use on the gang.

'Now, will you look at that?' Frankie's mum stopped calling Frankie names. She pointed in vexation at the old alarm clock by the side of her bed, 'They'll be here any minute and the table not yet laid! Just be a good girl and do what I ask.' She held out the dress, coaxing. 'Just for once, Frankie . . . please?'

She could have gone on fighting. If she'd fought hard enough, her mum would have backed off; everyone knew it wasn't wise to cross Frankie Foster. But you couldn't help feeling sorry for people sometimes. Like now, with her mum standing there, all skinny and flushed, pleading with her to wear the stupid dress. She was obviously desperate to impress the piggy-eyed slob. She was wearing one of her best on-the-razzle get-ups: a frilled nylon blouse, see-through (of course she had something on underneath), gold peep-toe sandals and a bright pink skirt, pencil slim, with a long sexy slit up one side. She had good legs, did Frankie's mum; she could wear things like that. She looked really smart, in the pink skirt.

'Please, Frankie,' she said, 'for me?'

'Oh, if I must.' Embarrassed by her own generosity, Frankie snatched ungraciously at the dress and began ramming her way into it.

'That's a girl!' Her mother nodded, approvingly. 'Just

take care you don't split it, now – and don't forget to put your shoes and socks on. I'll be out in the kitchen, gettin' things ready.'

Ready for Pig Eye. Slobby old Pig Eye. Frankie made a grunting, slob noise as she struggled with the dress.

'Ah, now, Frankie, just try to cheer up! Think of it this way: you're not losing a mother but gaining a father, and a little brother. What girl could ask for more?'

Frankie's head emerged, scarlet with rage and exertion, through the opening at the top of the dress. She didn't want a little brother! And she already had a father, somewhere.

In Jamaica, that was where she had a father. Frankie wished that she was in Jamaica. She bet in Jamaica you didn't have to go round in stupid red dresses with bits of lace all over them. She bet there it was so lovely and warm and sunny you could go round practically naked if you wanted. Not that she would, of course. She'd wear a pair of jeans, cut down to make shorts, with all the edges raggedy and frayed, the way she liked them, and a T-shirt saying 'Billie Small is a piggy-eyed slob'.

She *hated* Billie Small.

From out of the cardboard box where she kept all her treasures – 'Frankie B. Foster', it said. 'Private Property: Trespassers will be prosecuted' – Frankie took an old brown envelope addressed to Ms Theresa Kelly. Theresa Kelly was what her mum had been called before she had decided to become Mrs Foster. She always signed herself Mrs Foster even though strictly speaking she wasn't. (As she had told Frankie, not once but many times over, 'The bastard took off before I could manage to pin him down.')

The old brown envelope was so old that it was almost falling to pieces. Carefully, Frankie shook out the contents: a torn scrap of blue air letter, with writing; a Jamaican postage stamp, with a postmark dating from six years ago; and a photograph of a man rowing a boat on the Serpentine – Frankie's dad.

Originally her mum had been in the boat as well, but one day in a rage ('Horrid old cow!') Frankie had slashed her out with a pair of scissors. Just a bit of dress still showed: yellow, with white stripes. Frankie sometimes thought that she could remember that dress, though the photograph had been taken before she was even born. She had rescued it from a pile of rubbish on the day they had moved from their bedsitter to come and keep house for Mr Harding.

She knew the man was her dad, not just because he was black but because on the back, in her mum's scrawly writing, it said, 'Paul and Theresa on the Ser—' The rest had been cut off, but before it had been cut off it had said 'Serpentine', which was some water where people went rowing, in Hyde Park.

Frankie sat studying her photograph, as she had studied it lots of times before, usually when she was in need of comfort or reassurance. She was glad she took after her dad rather than her mum. She would have hated to have red hair and freckles, and skin the colour of skimmed milk that went all raw and painful if it caught the sun. Frankie's skin was dark, like her dad's. She had the same black hair, cropped very short, and the same brown eyes. (Her mum's were a sort of green-blue.) Billie Small had black hair and brown eyes, but his eyes were piggy and mean and his skin was indoor-grey. At least no one would ever take him for her dad; that was one consolation.

'Frankie Foster, what are you doing now?'

Frankie jumped, guiltily. 'Getting dressed, like you said.'

'I said to get those shoes and socks on . . . now get them on!' The shoes and socks came flying across the room towards her. At the same moment, the front-door bell rang. 'Heavens above! That'll be them!' Frankie's mum flew off again down the passage, shouting at Frankie as she went: 'You come out just as soon as you're ready, d'you hear?'

Frankie nodded, glumly. She put her dad back in his envelope, back in the cardboard box, back under the bed. Then she sat on the floor and thrust her feet into the white socks. The socks were knee-length; they had little pink rosebuds embroidered down the sides. The sandals were red, to go with the dress. They had long leather straps which fastened round the ankles. Little-girl stuff.

Frankie jumped on to the bed and looked at herself in the mirror: horrible! If the gang could see her now . . . well, the gang jolly well weren't going to see her! No one was going to see her, other than Piggy-eye Small and his soppy son. She wasn't going outside the house in this gear. She would be a laughing stock.

Her neck poked up like a giraffe's through the lacy neck hole of the little red dress. She wasn't made for little red dresses; she was a boy, really. She ought to have been a boy. She knew this, because once when she had asked her mother why she was called Frankie – Frankie Bernadette Foster, not Frankie-short-for-Frances as most people seemed to think, but Frankie all by itself – her mother had said that it was because her dad had wanted it. It had never seemed to occur to him, she'd said, that Frankie might turn out to be a girl.

'D'you think if I'd been a boy he'd have stayed with us?' Frankie had asked; but her mother had only pursed her lips and said she didn't know about that.

Frankie did. She knew. Her dad had gone back to Jamaica because she hadn't been what he'd wanted. He'd stuck around just long enough to be sure, just long enough to check that it wasn't a mistake, and then he'd gone. Her dad would be proud of her in her T-shirt and tracksuit, jumping out of trees. He wouldn't be proud of her in this stupid dress; he'd be dead ashamed of her.

17

Frankie plucked fretfully at the lace collar. Maybe if she could stuff the collar down inside the neck. . . .

'Are you not ready yet?' It was her mother at the door again. 'Get out here this instant! Tea's on the table and we're all waitin'!'

Shoulders hunched and chin sunk down as far as it would go, Frankie slouched after her mother along the passage. There in the kitchen, piggy eyed as ever, sat Billie Small. Next to him, looking like some undersized weed that had just struggled up for a bit of air, sat Jasper. He was small, even for a seven-year old. Not only was he small, he was sort of . . . shrivelled; sort of wizened – like a garden gnome. His head was all pointy, and so were his ears, and his neck wobbled like the stem of a flower.

'Frankie,' said her mother, 'this is Jasper. Jasper, this is Frankie, who's going to be your new sister.'

Jasper and Frankie glanced furtively at each other then quickly looked away again. I don't want to be anyone's sister, thought Frankie. Maybe Jasper didn't want to be anyone's brother. His eyes were all red and watery. He looked as if he had been crying; or as if he were about to cry.

'Isn't this nice?' beamed Frankie's mum. 'All the family gathered round?'

'Smashing,' said Billy. 'And afterwards –' He winked at Frankie's mum across the table. 'Who knows?'

Frankie's mum giggled. Frankie looked at her, crossly. She hated people giggling when she didn't know what they were giggling about. And afterwards –

Afterwards what? She supposed they were going to kiss and cuddle; her mum and Billie Small. It made Frankie feel quite sick.

2

Go out to play? 'But I've been out to play!'

'So who's a lucky girl?' said Pig Eye, with a wink.

Frankie, rather pointedly, turned her back on him. 'What do I want to go out again for? I want to watch the television!'

'You'll get square eyes, stuck in front of that box all day . . . you get and take Jasper over the Heath.'

She didn't want to take Jasper over the Heath; she'd been over the Heath. And how could she go out, dressed like this? Somebody might see her.

'I'll lend you my watch so you'll know when to be back. One hour, all right?'

'Why an hour?' said Frankie.

Her mum looked across at Billie Small. They giggled; like *school* children.

'Why an hour?' bellowed Frankie.

'Because I say an hour, that's why!'

They were having secrets. Frankie didn't like that. She stomped crossly up the basement steps, the gnome tagging along in the rear.

'*Secrets*,' she said. 'Keeping things from us.'

Of course, the gnome didn't care; he was too young. Probably too dopey, too. He hadn't said a word all through tea, and when Pig Eye had snarled at him to get his elbows off the table and, 'Keep your mouth shut when you're eating!' he'd gone all red, and looked as if he were about to start blubbing. Frankie had felt almost sorry for

19

him, until her mum had suddenly biffed at her and shouted, 'Yes, and you can keep your elbows off the table as well, Frankie Foster!' which hadn't been fair, because Frankie hadn't had her elbows on the table, and even if she had, so what? You had to put your elbows somewhere. You couldn't just leave them hanging around at your sides all the time.

She marched up Beechcroft Road, round the corner, down the High Street and on to the Heath. The gnome trotted obediently, in silence, at her heels.

'What d'you want to do?' said Frankie. If she'd had a piece of rope she could have tied it round his neck and pretended he was a dog. 'D'you want to climb a tree? I can show you a tree I've climbed that's higher, I bet, than anything you've ever seen ... d'you want to go and look at it?'

'Yes,' said the gnome.

It was almost the first word Frankie had heard him say. 'What do people call you?' said Frankie. 'They can't call you Jasper.' Jasper wasn't at all the sort of name for a garden gnome; Jasper was a name for someone tall and dark and sinister. 'What do they call you at school?'

'Don't call me nuffink.'

'So what do they say when they talk t'you, "Hey, you"?'

'Don't ever talk t'me.'

'Teachers've got to. They gotta talk t'you. What d'they call you?'

'Jasper Smaw.'

'Jasper Smaw?'

'Jasper Smaw.'

'You mean Small,' said Frankie. 'I'm not going to call you Jasper Small. Stupid name! I'm going to call you Jass. So when I say Jass, that's you, and you gotta do what I tell you.' He might as well get used to the idea – she was the one who was going to be boss. She tried it out, now. 'When I say run, you gotta run. RUN!'

He ran. He didn't run very fast – his feet were all splayed out and he lifted his legs too high – but at least he did it. Frankie was impressed. This was power! Not even the Gool or Toenail could be relied upon to obey instantly and without question.

'Stop!' shrieked Frankie. Jass stopped. He was panting, even though he'd only gone a few metres. He really was a weed. 'Turn right,' said Frankie. 'Keep straight on till you come to the fountain. When we get to the fountain I'll give you further instructions.'

Frankie was going to be prime minister when she grew up. She had already decided this. It was good giving people orders and knowing that they had to do whatever you said.

They reached the fountain and Frankie called out her new instructions: 'Turn left and keep on walking till I tell you to stop.'

Jass walked, obediently, two paces in front of the prime minister. It was his job to clear the way and make sure it was safe. Obviously, if you were prime minister, there were going to be all sorts of people who were jealous and wanted to do things to you. (Like that boy in Class 3 that had threatened to push her teeth in for being cheeky.) It was only right she should have a faithful servant to act as bodyguard.

'Stop!' shouted Frankie. Jass stopped. 'This is the tree that I climbed. See that branch?' She pointed. 'I jumped off of that.'

Jass looked up at it. Then he looked at Frankie. He put his thumb in his mouth.

'I s'pose you don't b'lieve me?' said Frankie. 'I s'pose you think I'm making it up? Well, I'll show you, if you like. D'you want me to show you?'

He nodded, though somewhat dubiously.

'You wait there,' said Frankie.

She had forgotten, until she started climbing, that she was wearing the stupid red dress and the sandals. Sandals weren't as good for climbing in as trainers; they kept slipping and sliding so that twice she nearly came off and scraped her hands and knees on the rough bark. She might have given up had she been on her own, but Frankie never admitted defeat in front of other people.

She reached the branch at last and heaved herself astride it. 'Hey!' She flapped a hand at Jass, a tiny pinpoint far below. Jass tilted his face up towards her. All she could see was the big black hole of his mouth wide open. Just for a minute Frankie wondered if this really was the same branch. The ground was miles away; it made her feel all quivery, just looking at it. It made her feel ill.

Down below, the black hole closed as a thumb was clamped in it.

'Do you want me to jump?' yelled Frankie. 'I will if you want.'

Silence.

'All right, then,' said Frankie, 'if you don't believe me—'

'Fwankee, *don't*!' screamed Jass.

Frankie sat for a moment, astride her branch. She wasn't one to admit defeat – but it wouldn't really be defeat; not in front of Jass. After all, he was only a garden gnome. Only a servant. And she'd proved that she *could* do it, if she wanted.

Slowly Frankie edged herself back to safety and began the long, slithery descent to the ground. It was even more difficult going down than it had been going up. She hung for a moment by her hands, seeking a final foothold before letting go and plummeting to earth. As she did so, there was a strange tearing sensation in her armpits. She wondered what it was. Whatever it was it didn't hurt, and her arms still seemed to be attached to her body, so it couldn't be anything much.

Nonchalantly, Frankie swung herself to the ground. Jass stood watching her, big-eyed.

'I didn't jump,' said Frankie, 'in case I landed on you . . . land on someone from that height, you could crush 'em. You saw how high it was, didn't you? 'bout a mile, I'd say, . . . a mile, easy. More like a mile'n a half, could be. I bet you ain't never jumped that far.'

She looked challengingly at him, but all he said was: 'You've tore your dwess.'

'Where? Where've I tore it?'

Silently, Jass pointed at Frankie's right armpit. 'It's all tored.'

Frankie lifted her right arm and peered gingerly beneath it. Then she lifted her left arm and peered beneath that. Horrors! Great gaping holes. That was going to mean a clip round the ear. But fancy going and buying something that all fell to bits when you just moved around in it! That wouldn't have happened if she'd worn her tracksuit. She'd always known that dresses were stupid things. Maybe if she kept her arms stuck down by her sides her mum wouldn't notice and she'd be able to pinch a needle and a bit of thread and sew it up again. Except that she wasn't terribly good at sewing. Miss Lacey, at school, had said she must have two left hands, whatever that meant. (If she really had two left hands she could go as an exhibit and be famous.)

Frankie decided that she wouldn't think about the torn armpits just for now. 'What d'you want to do next?' Her mother's watch, strapped halfway up her arm, showed twenty-five past five. They had another thirty minutes to go. What did you do with a seven-year old for a whole thirty minutes? Frankie tried to remember what she had done when she was seven years old, but it was such a long time ago ... three years, almost. She could hardly be expected to remember back that far. 'D'you want to go for a walk, or—'

'Make daisy chains.'

'Make *daisy* chains?'

'Wid daisies.' Jass, already, was scrabbling on the ground, plucking at things. Yellow things.

'They ain't daisies!' Even Frankie knew that. Daisies were white. 'They're dandelions ... make you wet your bed, they do.'

Jass puckered his face at her.

''s true,' said Frankie. 'You pick them, you'll widdle all over the bed, then your dad'll belt you.'

A look of terror appeared in Jass's eyes. He flung away the yellow flowers as if they were poison.

Don't say he'd actually believed her? 'You scared of your dad?' said Frankie.

The thumb went back into the open mouth.

'Does he wallop you?'

Jass said nothing; just slid his eyes away.

'My mum wallops me all the time – not fr wetting the bed, o'course.' He needn't think she did *that*. 'But fr other things ... like this, fr instance.' She held up her right arm and jabbed a finger into her armpit. 'She'd wallop me for that, all right; box my ears, prob'ly. That what your dad does t'you?'

Jass swallowed. Still he said nothing.

'Better not try it on me,' said Frankie. She didn't mind her mum bashing her, but she wasn't having old Pig Eye start coming on heavy. She'd jolly well give him what for if he did. 'Hey, look!' She knelt and pointed at a little patch of blue star-shaped flowers nestling in the grass. 'These is okay, we could make chains out of these. Come and help pick 'em. Show us what to do.'

They spent the rest of the time making daisy chains out

24

of the blue flowers. It was a fiddly sort of job. First you had to split the stem, but only enough to make a hole in it, not to shatter it completely; then you had to thread another stem through the hole; then you had to split that stem and thread another stem through that one. Frankie, who had chewed her nails till they were the merest stumps, wasn't much good at splitting, she was more of a shatterer, so Jass did the splitting while she did the threading. She wasn't all that good at threading, either. Jass was good at both. By the time the watch said six o'clock they had a whole long daisy chain of little blue flowers.

'What'll we do with it?' said Frankie.

'Puddit wounda neck.'

'Round *your* neck.' Frankie wasn't having any daisy chains round hers; it was bad enough having a lace collar. 'Here y'are . . . King Jasper. We c'n go home now. We bin out an hour.' She took his hand as they crossed the High Street. 'Wonder what they wanted us out the way for? Maybe they're making a surprise. Maybe it's presents.'

Frankie lived in hope of presents. Mr Harding quite often gave them to her; little bits of this and that that he'd picked up and thought she might like. 'Close your eyes and put your hands out,' he'd say. And then when she looked she'd find she was holding a woolly pencil case in the shape of a caterpillar, or a long wriggly snake made out of rubber. Once, and best of all, she'd found a pearl-handled penknife that had belonged to Mr Harding's grandmother. He never gave her soppy things like beads or bangles; he knew she wouldn't thank him for those.

'What d'you think it'll be? Treasure hunt? With presents at the end?'

Jass sucked his thumb; he looked doubtful.

'I bet it will!' said Frankie. 'I bet it'll be a treasure hunt and presents . . . what'd you have, if you could choose?'

Jass thought for a bit. Then, speaking through a mouthful of thumb, he said; 'Wolls Woyce.'

It took Frankie a second or so to translate: 'Rolls Royce?'

'Wolls Woyce motor.'

'Real one?'

'Modu one.'

'Model one. Okay, you have a Rolls Royce, I'll have . . .' She was about to say that she would have a bicycle, but that was stupid; nobody gave you things like bicycles. 'I'll have a chemistry set.' She'd wanted a chemistry set for ages. She wanted to learn how to make stink bombs. She had once read a book where all the kids in a class had let off stink bombs at exactly the same moment and the teacher had passed clean out with the stench. That was what Frankie wanted to do with her stink bombs, when she had learnt how to make them. 'I'll have this chemistry set,' she said, 'with all little bottles and test tubes and things. And powders for making bad smells.' She glanced at Jass, to see how he liked the idea, but he just went on sucking at his thumb. 'Smells,' said Frankie. 'Like – you know! When you . . .' She bunched her lips together and forced out a spurt of air. It was unmistakably a Rude Noise. Jass looked at her, saucer-eyed. 'Well, anyway,' said Frankie, 'that's what I'm gonna have . . . gonna have a chemistry set.'

She didn't really and truly expect there to be a chemistry set waiting for her, but she did have a faint hope that they might have been arranging some kind of a treat, because why else would they have wanted her and Jass out of the way? Once when Toenail had been told to 'Go out and play with your friends for a bit' there had been a brand new puppy waiting for him when he got back. Frankie wouldn't mind a puppy. A puppy wouldn't be half bad. She could teach it to play football and train it to sit, and stay, and walk to heel.

It was Pig Eye who opened the door to them. Frankie

bounced eagerly past, looking for signs of something exciting. She was so busy looking that she forgot about keeping her arms glued to her sides to hide her torn armpits. Her mother, coming out of the bedroom, stood stock still and shrieked, 'Frankie Foster, will you look at the state of you? Plastered in filth from head to toe! The ways of that girl are worse than those of a dung beetle!'

That was *before* she saw the armpits. When she saw the armpits she just went crazy.

Pig Eye left at half-past six, taking Jass with him. There wasn't any treat; there weren't any presents. All there was was Frankie's mum, going on about the mess she had made of herself. 'You could've worn that dress for the wedding! Now what am I to do, go out and buy another?'

Frankie, feeling a general sense of disgruntlement – tea with Pig Eye, *girl's clothes*, *NO PRESENTS* – kicked sullenly at the back door. 'Won't come to the wedding.'

'You'll do as you're told!'

'But I don't want to.'

'Well, you're going to.'

'Why?'

'Because I say so, that's why!'

'But I d—'

'Will you just stop your arguing!' Frankie's mum swung a punch. It was only half-hearted; Frankie didn't even bother to duck. 'You're coming to the wedding and that's that. Billie'll expect it.'

'Dunno what you want to get married to him for anyway.'

'And why shouldn't I get married to him?'

Frankie wanted to say, 'Because I hate him and he's horrible!' but she didn't quite dare. The next punch might be for real. She contented herself, instead, with kicking again at the back door. 'If you want to marry someone, why can't you marry Mr Harding?'

'Mr Harding?' Her mother gave a derisive hoot of laughter. 'That old goat!'

'If you married Mr Harding we could stay living here.'

'For your information, I don't want to stay living here! I don't want to spend the rest of my life stuck underground like a mole . . . I want a place of my own! You'll like it, where we're going. Billie has this fine new flat overlooking the park. Everything modern and up-to-date. Living here is like living in a morgue.'

'What's a mawg?'

'A place where they keep the dead bodies . . . dark; damp; dismal. Like this. . . .' Her mother waved a hand, up towards the ceiling (cracked and cobwebby) down to the floor (stone slabs, covered with old strips of carpet). 'It's disgusting, so it is! There'll be none of that at Billie's.'

'I bet Billie's isn't as big!'

'No, it's not, and who'd want it to be? The size of this place, it's like a barn. High time it was pulled down and flats put up. Twelve rooms just for one old man? It shouldn't be allowed.'

Her mother was always grumbling about Mr Harding living by himself in a house with twelve rooms. (Sixteen if you counted the basement, but that wouldn't be fair, because Frankie and her mother took up all the basement area.) Selfish, Frankie's mother said it was. Frankie didn't see what was selfish about it. After all, the house belonged to Mr Harding, so why shouldn't he live there? The Queen lived in Buckingham Palace, and that was oceans bigger. She knew the Queen didn't live all by herself, but she bet, even after space had been found for the servants and the Duke of Edinburgh, the Queen still had more than twelve rooms. *And* she had lots of other palaces she could go and live in. It wasn't fair, going on about Mr Harding. He was

28

probably quite lonely, having to live in all these rooms by himself.

Frankie had asked him about it once and he had said that he did sometimes get a bit lonely, and sometimes he agreed with Frankie's mother that it might be rather selfish. 'But I quieten my conscience by reflecting that I shall be dead pretty soon and then they can do with it as they will. Until then . . . there are too many ghosts.'

'*Ghosts*?' Frankie had said. 'Are there *ghosts*?'

'Oh, yes! Innumerable ones. But none that you need be scared of.'

Frankie wasn't scared! It was one of her greatest ambitions, to meet a ghost. She had spent ages searching, poking into dark corners, peering up the chimneys, but she hadn't yet managed to find one, in spite of Mr Harding claiming they were all about him. (She rather thought that one of them might be Mrs Harding, who had died in the first floor bedroom at the back, something Frankie knew from having listened to a conversation between her mother and the lady in the sweet shop.)

'Who'll look after things,' said Frankie, 'when we aren't here?'

'So long as it's not me,' said her mother, 'I couldn't care!' And then, seeing the expression on Frankie's face: 'He'll find someone, don't you worry! There'll be plenty queuing up to take our place.'

Frankie wasn't sure she liked the idea of other people taking their place – other people living in their basement. She wondered how Mr Harding felt about it. Nobody had consulted Mr Harding. Nobody had consulted Frankie, either. It had just been her mother and Pig Eye, just doing what they wanted; not caring about anyone else. They were the ones who were selfish.

Frankie wrenched, furiously, at the back door.

'And where might you be off to?' said her mother.

'Going into the garden.'

'Did I hear you ask?'

'Please can I go into the garden?'

'So long as you mind and behave, and don't make a nuisance of yourself.'

When Frankie's mum said don't make a nuisance of yourself, she meant don't climb over the fence and go talking to Mr Harding. She really hated Frankie talking to Mr Harding. Mr Harding didn't hate it; he was the one who usually called her over. He had said to her, once, that she reminded him of how his granddaughter had been, when she was Frankie's age. (Mr Harding's granddaughter was married now, and living in New Zealand, which meant that Mr Harding never saw her. His son was also living in New Zealand, which meant he never saw him, either. That was why he liked Frankie to go and talk to him: it stopped him feeling lonely. What was he going to do when Frankie wasn't there?)

Up the basement steps at the back was a small area of garden which had been fenced off from the rest. This was the part where Frankie's mum could hang out her washing and where Frankie could practise her judo and her commando course. Today, because she was busy thinking of other things, she didn't bother with the commando course but ran straight up to the fence to look for Mr Harding. He was out on the lawn, sitting in his favourite chair, doing his crossword, wearing his old white sun hat and his carpet slippers. There was a small table at his side with a glass containing whisky. Mr Harding drank one bottle of whisky a week: Frankie's mum had to buy it for him from the supermarket. She grumbled about it quite a lot. She didn't think it was right that Mr Harding should spend money on bottles of whisky. But it was his money: he could spend it on whatever he liked.

Frankie hung over the fence, humming rather loudly to herself, rocking to and fro in time to the humming. After a bit, Mr Harding lowered his paper and looked across at her. 'Coming over?' he said.

Frankie was over almost before the words were out of his mouth.

'And how is the world treating Frankie?' said Mr Harding.

Frankie pulled one of her faces; one of the hideous ones that she was noted for.

'Not treating her too well, eh?' Mr Harding spread his paper over his knees and laid his silver propelling pencil on the top of it. It was his special pencil that he used for doing crosswords. 'What's the problem? Want to tell me?'

Frankie scowled, and reached out for the pencil. 'It's her.'

'Her?' said Mr Harding.

'Getting married ... what's she want to get *married* for?'

'People do, you know.'

'Not at her age!'

'Come, come, come!' said Mr Harding. 'Just how old do you think your mother is?'

'I dunno.' Frankie shrugged. 'Fifty, maybe?'

'Fifty!' Mr Harding rocked silently in his chair. Frankie's scowl intensified. She twiddled with the knob at the end of the pencil, making the lead move up and down. 'Your mother's nowhere near fifty! She's still a young woman, hardly out of her teens. It's only natural she would want to get married.'

Frankie stood frowning, twiddling the pencil, wrestling with the idea of her mother being young. Certainly her hair wasn't white, it was still a bright, flaming red, and as far as Frankie knew she didn't have the sort of teeth that came out, like Mr Harding's did; but even so. . . .

'If she wants to get married, why can't she marry you?'

'Oh, my goodness! I don't think she'd care for that.'

'Why not?'

'Because I'm old.'

Frankie looked at Mr Harding carefully, from under her lashes. She supposed he was quite old. 'Are you more than fifty?'

'A lot more than fifty!'

'More'n sixty? More'n seventy? More'n eighty?' Frankie stopped, awestruck: more than eighty *was* old.

'If I were to live for another four years,' said Mr Harding, 'I should be more than ninety.'

'*Ninety?*' Frankie had never known anyone who was ninety. 'If you live ten years after that you'd be a hundred.'

'Oh, I shan't live to be a hundred! I shan't even live to be ninety.'

'Why not?' said Frankie. 'Are you going to die?'

'Almost certainly,' said Mr Harding. He didn't sound too upset about it. 'But I'll tell you what –' he reached for ward and took back his silver pencil '– when I die I shall leave you this in my will. Would you like that?'

'Yes, please!' Frankie's eyes glowed. To be left something in a will! That was like in olden times, like she'd seen on the television – everyone gathered round the death bed, with people quarrelling about who was going to get what. Except that in Frankie's case there wouldn't be anything to quarrel about, because Mr Harding was going to leave it to her specially, and it would be written down, for all to see, 'I leave my silver pencil to Frankie Bernadette Foster'.

'You will remember that it's Frankie,' she said, anxiously, 'not short for Frances?'

'What's that?' Mr Harding's attention had already wandered off elsewhere, as sometimes it had a habit of doing. He had picked up his paper and was frowning again at his crossword. 'Two down . . . a saint with a container. . . .'

'My name,' said Frankie. If he called her Frances they might try saying he'd meant someone different and then she would be done out of things. 'You got to put Frankie.'

'That's it! Franciscan!' Mr Harding beamed triumphantly at her. 'I've been after that one all day! A saint with a container: Francis-can.' He wrote it in, with a flourish, with Frankie's silver pencil. 'Stupid of me! Staring me in the face. Obvious when you know. Let's see, now, what does that give us? Three down . . . what do you think three down could be? Pitch one's tent, about a pound . . . what's another word for "pitch one's tent"? Come along, now! Put your thinking cap on; I need some help.'

Frankie stayed in the garden, helping Mr Harding ('camp' she suggested for 'pitch one's tent'; and it was!) until her mother shouted up at her from the basement steps that it was time for her to go in.

'Bed?' said Mr Harding.

'Not *yet*,' said Frankie. 'I expect she wants me to do something; do the ironing or something. She's always wanting me to do things.'

'Off you go, then! Mustn't keep her waiting.'

Frankie turned; then turned back again. 'You won't forget about it, will you?' she said. 'The pencil. In your will.'

'I won't forget,' said Mr Harding. 'I promise.'

3

A woman had come; she was called Mrs Gedge. She was immensely tall, and very cross looking, with black hair and red lips and eyes as hard as pebbles. Mrs Gedge was going to take over as housekeeper when Frankie's mum had married Billie Small and gone off with him to live in his flat. Frankie didn't like her. Frankie's mum said, 'Oh, well, you wouldn't. You never like anyone.'

That wasn't true: Frankie liked lots of people. She liked Hake and the Gool and Toenail. She liked Mr Harding. It was terrible to think of Mr Harding being taken care of by a cross-looking woman like Mrs Gedge. And then there was Donna. Donna Gedge was the same age as Frankie. She had black hair and red lips just like her mother, but whereas Mrs Gedge was thin, Donna Gedge was fat. Frankie hated fat people. Her mother said that Donna probably couldn't help being fat, it was probably something to do with her glands, but Frankie knew better. Donna Gedge was fat because she ate too much. Frankie had watched her guzzling up the biscuits when Mrs Gedge had come down to inspect the kitchen and had stayed to drink a cup of coffee. She had eaten every single one of the strawberry wafers; Frankie hadn't even got a look in, even though they were her favourites. If Frankie had pigged like that she'd have got a clip round the ear and been told to mind her manners, but nobody had said a word to Donna. Frankie could hardly bear the thought of that disgusting fat thing playing in *her* garden, hanging over *her* fence, talking to *her* Mr Harding.

Suppose – a fearsome thought suddenly struck her – suppose Donna saw the silver pencil? Suppose Mr Harding went and left it to her, instead of to Frankie? She knew that he had promised; but Frankie didn't set much store by grown-ups' promises. Miss Morris at school had once promised a prize for the person who could make the most words out of the word 'carpet', and Frankie had made thirty-two, which was loads more than anyone else, and Miss Morris had never given her her prize. That was because Miss Morris didn't like her. She said that she and Hake were bad influences. Frankie had once overheard her telling the teacher from Class 3 that, 'They come from broken homes, of course,' which had puzzled her for a long time, because although the basement ceiling at number 12 was a bit cracked it certainly wasn't broken.

It was Toenail who had explained to her what broken home meant. 'Means you haven't got a dad. Be all right when your mum gets married . . . you'll be a proper family then.'

If being a proper family meant living in Worple Park with Billie Small, Frankie thought she would rather stay broken.

The red dress had been put back together again and Frankie had got to wear it for the wedding. It wasn't the least bit of use arguing: her mother was determined. 'You're coming to the wedding and you're going to wear the dress. That's flat and final. I don't want to hear another word.'

'Do I get a present?' said Frankie.

'Do you get a present? I like your cheek! I'm the one getting married: I'm the one gets the presents! It's you ought to be buyin' one for me, my girl!'

'Presents for getting married?' It struck Frankie as

35

being decidedly unfair. What did her mother want a present for? She was getting Billie Small! It was Frankie who needed the present, to make up for having to move and leave all her friends behind. She asked Mr Harding about it, and he said, 'Oh, good gracious me, yes! Yes, indeed! Everybody gives you things when you get married.'

'What sort of things?'

'Oh! Something for the house . . . sheets. Pillow cases. Set of saucepans. Anything domestic.'

Anything domestic seemed very boring to Frankie. She wouldn't want anything domestic. She would rather have something like her chemistry set. On the other hand, Frankie's mum wasn't Frankie, and one had to allow for other people's peculiar tastes. Her mum, for example, liked china ornaments. Frankie couldn't stand them; they got in the way when you dusted (dusting being one of Frankie's most hated tasks) and more often than not they fell on the floor and got broke, and then you got a biff round the ear and a mouthful of abuse. But her mum liked them, and if you were going to buy people presents then you ought to buy them something they liked.

After much deliberation – much picking up and putting down and fingering of the goods, which caused the lady behind the ornament counter to frown and make tutting noises – Frankie chose a china cart pulled by a china donkey wearing a straw hat, with his ears poking out of the top. It cost more than she had really wanted to spend, but maybe if she gave her mum a china donkey then when it came to Frankie's birthday her mum might actually, at long last, give her her chemistry set. She'd jolly well better.

Mr Harding's wedding present was a big blue bowl with white figures doing a sort of dance all round the outside of it. Frankie's mum was in raptures. She said it was something called Wedgewood and that it must have cost a fortune.

Olive gave her an electric carving knife, which had Frankie in raptures. An electric carving knife looked to her exactly like the sort of weapon a commando might use. Her mother said she didn't know about commandos, but Frankie could just keep well away from it unless she wanted her bottom smacked. She said that Frankie could keep away from the Wedgewood, as well. 'It's far too valuable for a butter fingers like you to go pawing at it.'

'Is it more valuable than my donkey?'

'Well, put it this way – it cost a lot more.'

'My donkey cost ever such a lot.'

'I'm sure it did, and to me the donkey's just as valuable as the Wedgewood, but you can still keep away from it!'

The wedding was planned for a Friday. Frankie was supposed to be at school, and if she wasn't going to be at school then she needed a note to say why. In fact she needed a note for the whole of the rest of term, because the week after the wedding was honeymoon week, when her mother and Billie Small were going off to Clacton. Jass and Frankie were going to go with them. (They had to go, because there wasn't anyone they could be left with: Olive was working, and Billie Small's best mate, that was coming to the wedding, 'lived in' at the nuthouse and was, presumably, a nut. Must be to be best mates with Billie Small.)

After the honeymoon there was still another week of school to go before the summer holidays started, but nobody seemed to care. As Frankie's mum said, she would be going to a new school in September anyway, so what did it matter?

'But two weeks,' said Frankie, 'I'm gonna miss two weeks!'

'Two weeks is neither here nor there.'

Frankie wasn't so sure. Sometimes, in the past, she and Hake had played truant together, chasing up to the Heath or jumping on the tube and seeing where it took them; but that had been with Hake. This would be with Billie Small. And if she didn't go back to school for the end of term it might mean she would never see any of them again. Hake, and the Gool, and Toenail . . . they had been with each other since the beginning.

'Don't you fret,' said Frankie's mum. 'You'll forget about them soon enough. Easy come, easy go; that's the way of it. You'll miss them for a day or two, maybe, then you'll find someone else and it'll be just as if they never were.'

'Was that how it was with my dad?' said Frankie.

'Was what how it was with your dad?'

'When he went back to J'maica, did you miss him for a day or two, then find someone else?'

'Are you deliberately being cheeky?' Frankie's mum aimed a blow. Frankie skipped sideways. She felt indignant: she hadn't been being cheeky! She had genuinely wanted to know.

'What was he like?'

'He was scum!'

'So why did you get to be friends with him?'

'Because I was a fool and too young to know better and he sweet-talked me. Just like they all do.'

'What, even *him*?' She couldn't bring herself to refer to Billie Small as Billie. She certainly wasn't ever going to call him Dad. Jass could make believe, if he wanted. He could call Frankie's mum 'Mum' and pretend that she really was. Frankie wasn't going to pretend. 'Did *he* sweet-talk you?'

'If you mean Billie, he most certainly did! But Billie's different; he's a mature man, and he's got a good steady job. Your precious father never did an honest day's work

38

in his life – just an idle layabout. The best thing that ever happened to me was him walking out.'

Frankie's mum had once said that it was the worst thing that had ever happened to her. Frankie wished she would make her mind up.

'Wonder what he's doing now?'

'It won't be anything to write home about, I can tell you that! Only one place that man was heading, and that was the gutter. And just stop your impertinence!' Her mother hit out again. This time, Frankie wasn't quite quick enough: the blow caught her on the ear. 'You think I want to hear talk about that man on the eve of my wedding? You do it just to aggravate!'

'I don't!' howled Frankie, clutching her ear. 'I wanna know!'

'Know what? That he was a good-for-nothing? A wastrel? Didn't care tuppence for his own flesh and blood? At least Billie's willing to put a roof over your head. That's a sight more than your precious father ever did! You just get in that bedroom, now, and get yourself into bed. We've to be up early tomorrow, the ceremony's at ten-thirty and I don't want any trouble.'

Frankie, still clutching her ear, clumped sullenly off to the bedroom. Stupid wedding. Stupid ceremony. Stupid red dress, hanging over a chair. She hated her mother for marrying Billie Small. She hated Billie Small. She didn't want him to put a roof over her head. She didn't believe her own dad hadn't cared tuppence; he'd just been disappointed that she wasn't a boy. And that was probably her mother's fault. She bet there were things you could do to make babies into boy babies or girl babies. Things like chucking salt over your shoulder or not eating sardines. She bet there were, if you really wanted. Obviously her mother hadn't really wanted. And now she was marrying that horrible creep. Frankie felt like screaming.

Instead, she pulled out her cardboard treasure box

from beneath her bed, opened it up and took out the photograph. All the rest of her possessions had been packed into suitcases and plastic sacks and been taken off to Worple Park by Billie Small in a hired van, but Frankie wasn't letting her precious treasure box go off in any van.

The man rowing his boat on the Serpentine looked up at Frankie and smiled. (She knew he wasn't really smiling, he'd just had the sun in his eyes when the photograph was taken, but she liked to pretend that it was a smile. She liked to pretend that he could see her, as she was now, dressed in her tracksuit and looking like a boy; he would be proud of her if he could see her now.)

'Don't worry,' said Frankie, to the photograph, 'you're my real dad, not him. He'll never be.'

The door was thrown open and her mother came in.

'Frankie Foster—' She stopped. 'What's that you've got there?'

'It's mine!' Frankie clutched the photograph to her chest.

'What is it? If it's some of that rude stuff they leave over the Heath—'

'It's not rude stuff!'

'So what is it?' Before Frankie could stop her, her mother had crossed the room and snatched at the photograph. She gave a scornful hoot of laughter as she saw what it was. 'That old thing! I thought I threw that out years ago?'

'It's mine!' Frankie clawed desperately at it. 'You don't want it! Give it me!'

'Oh, you can have it! You're welcome.' Contemptuously, her mother tossed the photograph back at her. It hung for a moment in mid-air, then slowly fluttered floorwards. Frankie caught at it just in time. 'Oh, yes, he was a fine figure of a man in those days. Just don't go kiddin' yourself he'd look like that now!'

I bet he would, thought Frankie. I bet he jolly well would.

The wedding wasn't at all how Frankie had expected a wedding to be. She had known it wouldn't be as grand as a royal wedding, like she'd seen on the television, but she had thought it would happen in a church and that there would be music and hymns and lots of people.

'People?' said her mother. 'What people?'

'People that go to weddings!'

'You have to know them first,' said her mother. 'I don't know anyone, do I?'

'Did Prince Andrew know all the people that went to his wedding?'

'I daresay he did. He hasn't been kept living underground like a mole all these years. He's been able to get out and do things.'

'P'raps—' Frankie suggested it hopefully: all might not be lost even at this late hour – 'p'raps you should've waited till you'd been able to get out and do things, then you'd've known people. P'raps you ought to put it off till next year, or—'

'Put it off? Will you listen to the child! Put it off, she says. This could be the only chance that ever comes my way!'

Only chance of what? thought Frankie, sourly. Marrying Billie Small?

Her mother, who had been standing at the top of the basement steps, suddenly turned and made impatient beckoning motions. 'Here's the car, now! Hurry along!'

As part of his wedding present, Mr Harding had hired a special white wedding car to take them to the Register Office and bring everybody back again afterwards. Mr Harding wasn't coming to the actual ceremony – he said he was too decrepit, his joints would start creaking and embarrass everyone – but he had promised to drink their health later, at what Billie Small called 'the knees-up'. (Frankie's mum giggled when he called it this. She said he was awful, and that it wasn't a knees-up, it was a reception. In spite of hating Billie Small, Frankie couldn't help feeling that a knees-up sounded as if it might have a bit more going for it: reception sounded like school.)

The only people at the Register Office were Olive and Billie Small's mate from the nuthouse. Billie Small was there, of course, with the garden gnome. The garden gnome was wearing a suit that was several sizes too big for him and his eyes were redder than ever.

'You bin crying?' said Frankie, as they all stood round in a room like a dentist's waiting room, waiting for the man that married people to come and marry Billie Small and Frankie's mum.

'He was stupid,' said Billie Small, 'plain stupid. Gets my goat, sometimes, how stupid that boy can be.'

'Poor little feller!' said Frankie's mum. She held out her arms, but the gnome wouldn't go to her because of Billie Small standing there. Frankie didn't blame him. She bet when Billie Small whacked, he really did whack. He had these big meaty hands like sides of beef and although he wasn't very tall his shoulders were so broad that sometimes, if a door wasn't quite wide enough, he had to go through sideways. She looked at him, glowering. He'd just better not try any of his whacking on her.

'Wanna play something?' Frankie turned to the gnome, thinking that perhaps a game would cheer him up. Not only that, she was growing bored, standing about in the waiting room. There weren't even any magazines to look at. 'Race you down the corridor! Give you a start of ten. One—'

'Don't!' screamed Frankie's mum. Jass, who hadn't even moved, cringed deeper into the depths of his oversized suit.

'For goodness' sake,' said Olive, 'can't that girl ever

behave herself? This is your mum's wedding day, Frankie Foster! Just show a bit of respect.'

It wasn't Frankie's fault that a vase of flowers fell off the table and splattered water all over everywhere just as they were all going through to the marrying room. Olive said it was, but it jolly well wasn't. Frankie hadn't been anywhere near the rotten flowers.

'Jostling!' said Olive.

'I was not jostling! I was—'

'Shut your row!' said Frankie's mum.

The man who did the marrying was very solemn. He asked Frankie's mum whether she was Mary Theresa Kelly, of 12 Beechcroft Road, and then he asked Billie Small whether he was William Colin Small of Flat 8, Worple Court (checking, Frankie supposed, in case he went and married the wrong people – though you'd have thought, if he'd tried to do that, that the people would've stopped him). Next he asked them both if they had considered this step that they were taking; and finally, when they said that they had, and everybody except Jass and Frankie had written their names in a book, he told them that they were now man and wife and ordered Billie Small to give Frankie's mum a kiss, which to Frankie's unspeakable disgust he did.

The kiss went on and on, and they all had to stand there and watch. It was horrible. Olive kept making soppy baby noises, gurgling and cooing in her throat, and Billie Small's mate pulled a nutty face and made rude gestures (Frankie knew they were rude because Hake had told her) and after a bit yelled 'Time's up! Time's up! Knock it off!' Mercifully they did, because if they hadn't, Frankie rather thought she might have been sick. That creep, slobbering over her mum; it was grotesque!

Afterwards, outside, on the steps of the Register Office, they were allowed to throw confetti ('Not in people's eyes, you stupid child!') and Olive and Billie Small's best mate took photographs; some just of Billie Small and Frankie's mum, some of Frankie and Jass as well. Olive kept saying, 'Smile! Smile! Try and look happy!' and Frankie obligingly twisted her lips into a grimace (you had to smile when you were having your photograph taken, didn't you?) but Jass just kept staring at the ground until at last, in tones of exasperation, Olive cried, 'Try taking his hand, won't you, Frankie? See if that'll make him look a bit less miserable!'

Jass seemed to find comfort in having his hand held. He wouldn't let Frankie let go even after the photographs had all been taken and they had piled into the wedding car to go back to Beechcroft Road for the reception. He was a frightful weed, but she supposed he couldn't help it.

The knees-up was held in Mr Harding's big front room. It was like a sort of party, and was much more fun than the wedding. For a start, there were more people. There was the lady from the sweetshop, and the lady from the hardware store, and a lady from the checkout at the local supermarket, and some friends of Billie Small's, and of course Mr Harding. There was also Mrs Gedge and Donna, who were moving into the basement that same morning and had been invited upstairs to join in the celebrations. Frankie could have done without them. She kept a jealous eye on Donna, prepared to rush over at a moment's notice if she showed any signs of sucking up to Mr Harding, but Donna stuck with her mother, so that was all right.

Then there was the food; lots and lots of it. What was good was that you could just go on taking whatever you wanted. Nobody bothered telling you not to snatch or gobble. Nobody said that this would make you sick or that that wasn't suitable. Frankie tried everything she could lay her hands on. She made sure that Jass got his share, too. (Donna was pigging away in a corner, as hard as she could go.)

44

'Here!' Frankie would say, thrusting a sausage roll at him. 'Have a bash at this . . . try a bite of that. Fancy some of that wobbly stuff? Blermonge, that is. Pink blermonge.' Actually it was spelt blancmange on the packets that her mother used, but after years of thinking of it as blonkmonge Frankie had learned that the 'blonk' was pronounced 'bler'. That was because it was a foreign language. She tried explaining this to Jass – she saw it as part of her duty to educate him – but Jass was busy stuffing his cheeks with sausage rolls and crisps. He ate very fast, like a squirrel, jaws munching up and down, click-click-click, and one wary eye on Billie Small across the room. Billie Small didn't even look at him; he was showing off in front of his mates and couldn't have cared less. Frankie and Jass could eat just as much as they liked.

They gorged until they could gorge no more. It was the best blow out Frankie had ever had. She could almost feel the red dress straining at the seams.

All the grown-ups were drinking champagne. Some of the grown-ups were drinking rather a lot of champagne; Olive, for example. Olive had reached the stage of screeching very loudly, and giggling at absolutely everything. She kept draping herself round the neck of Billie Small's best mate, who just stood there, beaming and glistening and mopping at his face with a big yellow handkerchief.

Billie Small's mate had, as a matter of fact, been a bit of a disappointment to Frankie. She had thought, as he lived in the nuthouse, that he must be one of the nuts. She had told Hake and the others: 'We've got this nutter coming to my mum's wedding; a real live nutter out the nuthouse.' She had tried to imagine what a real live nutter would look like, how he would behave. She had had secret hopes of him suddenly running amok with the carving knife, or stripping off his clothes and making gibbering noises like a monkey, because that was the sort of thing that nuts did, wasn't it? It was what they did on the films. She had watched him closely all the time at the Register Office, looking for signs of nuttiness (his left ear kept twitching: that had got to be nutty) and then when they had arrived back at Beechcroft Road her mother had gone and introduced him to Mr Harding and Frankie heard her say, 'This is John, who works on the same ward as Billie.'

Frankie was disgusted – just another nut nurse! Grown-ups always let you down.

At two o'clock Frankie's mum came over and told Frankie to go to the lavatory, and to make sure that Jass went, too, because, 'We've got to be leaving in five minutes.' They were allowed, as it was a special occasion, to use Mr Harding's downstairs cloakroom, where a special guest towel had been put out. Jass and Frankie crammed in there together, and Frankie went all right, but Jass was shy and couldn't do it, so she had to go and wait for him outside, and still he couldn't do it. Frankie kept rattling the handle and calling, 'Have you been yet?' She wished he would hurry, she wanted to say goodbye to Mr Harding before they left. She wanted to remind him again about the pencil.

'Look, come on!' bellowed Frankie, hammering at the door. 'If you don't get a move on we'll go without you!'

Jass came out then, in a great rush, looking scared.

'Did you go?' said Frankie.

He said that he had, but she knew he was lying. That meant he'd probably piddle himself on the way to the station, and then he'd be walloped, and Frankie's mum would clip her round the ear and say that it was her fault.

Frankie stomped off in search of Mr Harding. She found him sitting in his chair in the back room, by the French windows.

'Are you off? I'm afraid the merriment got rather too much for me. Come and kiss me goodbye!' Mr Harding held out his arms: Frankie ran into them. 'You won't forget me, will you?' said Mr Harding. Frankie shook her head; her throat had suddenly swollen up and gone all funny and tight. 'You must send me a postcard, you know, and you must come back and visit me. You'll do that, won't you?'

Frankie nodded, vigorously.

'They've been a good few years, haven't they? Eh? We've had some good times, you and I; all those crosswords we've solved! I don't know how I'm going to manage without your help. Look at this, now, five down. Sniff and whimper . . . what d'you make of that?'

Frankie couldn't immediately make anything of it. She might have done, if she'd been given time – she was getting really good at crosswords – but her mother appeared before she had a chance to get to grips with it.

'Frankie!' she said. 'We'll miss that train. Thanks ever so much, Mr Harding, for all you've done. It's been really appreciated. I just hope the new woman gives satisfaction. Frankie, will you get on, now! And stop that sniffing. If you've got to sniffle, then use your handkerchief. What's the matter with you? Are you getting a cold, or something?' Grumbling, she pushed Frankie out of the door ahead of her. 'That's all we need; you down with a cold when we're trying to enjoy a honeymoon!'

It was only later, sitting on the train that was taking them to Clacton, that Frankie remembered: she had clean forgotten about the silver pencil.

4

They stayed in a real hotel in Clacton. It was called the Wellesley Court, and it was run by a lady called Mrs Pac Pomanarcki, which was an odd sort of name, but her husband had been Polish. Billie Small said that Pac Pomanarcki was far too difficult and that he was going to call her Mrs Plastic Mac. He could be quite funny when he wasn't being a creep.

Frankie had never stayed in a hotel before. She had thought that in hotels people would have rooms of their own and was a bit put out to discover that she was going to have to share with Jass, though Jass was happy. He said, 'This is nice, isn't it, Fwankee?' and beamed at her as he bounced up and down on his bed, so that she hadn't the heart to say she thought it was horrid. Not that it actually *was* horrid, it was just that she was sick of having to share bedrooms: she wanted a place that was hers.

When she asked her mother about it, her mother said, 'Ah, now, Frankie, for goodness' sake! You've only been here five minutes, don't start your moaning already. The wee feller can't get off to sleep by himself, he's afraid of the dark. In any case, two rooms cost twice the price of one.'

Frankie consoled herself with the reflection that it was only for a week. However loathsome Worple Park might be, she would at least have a room to herself.

It rained almost the whole of the time they were in Clacton. Mrs Plastic Mac said what a shame it was, 'Such a

48

disappointment for the kiddies,' but rain was something Frankie didn't mind. You could still go down to the beach and dig holes and watch them fill with water, or potter about amongst the rock pools searching for shrimps; and then, if the rain got too heavy, there was always the pier – provided you had the money. After the second day, Frankie always had the money.

It didn't rain on the day they got there, and it didn't rain on the second day, which was Sunday, so immediately after breakfast they all went down to the beach and Frankie's mum and Billie Small sat in deck chairs to read their Sunday newspapers whilst Jass and Frankie, in their swimsuits, went down to the water's edge to paddle and look for crabs.

After a bit, Frankie's mum came to tell them that she and Billie were going back to the hotel. 'We'll see you at lunch time . . . that's at twelve thirty. I'll come down here and fetch you. Until then, you stay on the beach and look after Jasper. All right?'

Frankie nodded. She didn't mind; she was quite happy, dibbling about in the water, dredging up bits of seaweed and tiny little crabs the size of five pence pieces.

'Don't you move from this spot, then. I don't want to have to spend hours searching for you.'

Frankie's mum went off with Billie Small; Frankie and Jass stayed where they were, shrieking and yelling as the waves rolled over them, swallowing gallons of salt water, getting it in their eyes and down their ears and up their noses.

'Look, I can swim!' cried Frankie, squatting down in the sea and making swimming motions with her arms.

'So can I, so can I!' screamed Jass, bobbing up and down with one foot touching the bottom.

'I can float!'

'So can I!'

'I can do the back stroke!'

49

'So can I!'

Jass did everything that Frankie did. Frankie scrambled on to a breakwater and jumped into the sea: so did Jass. Frankie found a piece of popping weed and started popping it: so did Jass. It was a great responsibility, being with someone who did everything that you did. But of course it was all part of being prime minister and having power.

'Let's look for things,' said Frankie. Toenail, who was the only one of the gang who regularly went away for holidays, had once come back from Broadstairs with the skeleton of a dogfish. Frankie would give anything to have a skeleton like that. They didn't manage to find a skeleton, but they did find a dead starfish with one of its fingers missing. Frankie waved it aloft in triumph. 'Let's go and show Mum!'

She set off at a gallop up the beach. It took her several seconds to realize that Jass wasn't with her. She turned, and shouted at him. 'Come on!'

Obediently, he stumbled after her, but she could see he wasn't happy.

'What's the matter?'

'She said we got to wait. She said she was going to come and fetch us.'

'Oh, poof!' Frankie swung her starfish, dismissing the objection. She was prime minister: she didn't have to hang around to suit other people's convenience. Anyway, she was starving; it must be nearly lunch time. 'We'll prob'ly bump into her on the way ... save her a journey.'

They didn't bump into her, the reason being that it was still only half-past eleven when they arrived back at the hotel. Frankie couldn't believe there was another hour to go until lunch: she was *starving*.

'Let's go and find them.' Maybe, if they were in a good mood, they would give her some money and she could go back up to the sea front and get an ice cream from one of the ice cream booths. She'd spent all her own money the first day here, buying a bucket and spade and mountains of candy floss. Then there'd been the donkey with the straw hat. If she hadn't bought the donkey she'd be pounds better off. 'Let's see if they're in the lounge!'

The lounge was where the television set was, and where people went after dinner to drink coffee: it was empty. So was the sun room. There was only one other place they could be, and that was in their bedroom.

With Jass trailing reluctantly behind, Frankie went thudding up the stairs, leaving little piles of sand on every step. Her mother and Billie Small had the first bedroom on the right. (She and Jass were next door, in a poky little place the size of a cupboard with just space enough for two divan beds and a small bedside table, with a shelf above for putting things on.)

'Mum?' Frankie crashed the door open, excitedly waving her dead starfish by one of its four remaining fingers. 'Look what we got! We got a—'

She stopped. Her mother was lying in bed, clutching the bedclothes to her chin. She looked alarmed, as if Jass and Frankie might be burglars come to rob her. Billie Small was out of bed. He had his back turned, and was pulling on his knickers. Frankie could see his bare bum, all hairy and pimpled. Heavens! What a sight!

Frankie turned and ran. Jass ran with her. They shot into their own room, where Frankie collapsed on to the nearest bed, giggling fit to bust. Jass stood awkwardly, finger in his mouth, waiting for her to finish. Frankie hiccuped and took her head out of the pillow. She looked up at Jass. 'Your dad's got a hairy bum!'

It was enough to set her off again. The giggles spurted out of her, exploding in muffled *crumps* into the pillow. Jass watched, helplessly.

'Frankie?' Her mother had come into the room. She sounded cross. She was wearing her silk kimono with the red dragon and the fringes, which she had bought for herself as a going away present. 'Do we have to pin a notice on our bedroom door saying "Please knock before entering"?'

Frankie sat up and wiped her eyes. 'I wanted to show you this!'

'What is it?'

'It's a starfish. It's got—'

'Throw it away, it looks horrible. And I don't care what you wanted to show me, just mind your manners and knock in future!'

'But it's a starfish.' She was going to put it in her treasure box. 'A starfish with four legs; could be valuable.'

'It's dirty. It'll rot and start to stink.'

'I'll wrap it in silver paper. C'n I have some money for an ice cream?'

'No, you certainly cannot! It'll be lunch time before we know where we are.'

'But I'm starving! So's Jass – aren't you?' She looked pointedly at him. Jass chewed his finger. 'We're both starving.'

'Yes, and if you eat ice creams now you won't eat your lunch later. Billie's paid for those lunches. I'm not having them wasted. And why didn't you stay on the beach like I told you? Didn't I tell you? *Stay on the beach*. . . . Come back here, bursting in on people—'

'What was you in bed for?' said Frankie.

'Because I felt tired, that's why! Grown-ups get tired. Life's not all play for us, you know; not like it is for you kids. So you just remember, another time . . . you knock before coming into our room.'

Frankie frowned, balancing her four-fingered starfish on the palm of her hand. 'Didn't have to knock before.'

'Frankie –' her mother turned, exasperated, 'things are

52

different now.' She wrenched the door open. 'I'm *married*.'

Huh! Frankie sat brooding, looking down at her starfish. Just because Billie Small had a hairy bum, that was all it was. A big hairy bum that he was ashamed of people seeing. She'd be ashamed if she had a bum like that. Hairs and pimples – *yuck*.

A sudden noise made her jump. What was that? She looked round, quickly. Jass had taken his finger from his mouth and left his jaw hanging open. It made him look half witted.

The noise came again. This time, Frankie recognized it: it was voices. Loud voices, raised in anger. They were coming from the room next door. Frankie sprang up from her bed.

'Fwankee—' Jass was trembling.

'Shudd up!' said Frankie. She pressed her ear to the wall, straining to catch the odd word.

'But Fw—'

'Shudd *up*!'

The wall was too thick. Carefully, she eased open the bedroom door, crawled on hands and knees into the passage, shuffled a few yards, rose up to keyhole height and tried again. This time, she could hear Billie Small's voice, quite clearly. What she heard was: '. . . that poxy brat of yours!'

Then her mother, in reply: 'She wasn't to know. She's not used to having a man about the place.'

'Well, she'd better get used to it, and damn quick, if she doesn't want to be on the receiving end of my hand!'

'Ah, now, Billie!' (Her mother, placating.) 'Don't be like that! You promised!'

Then there was a low growling, which Frankie couldn't make out, ending with a: 'Bloody kids! Who needs 'em?'

'Billie! Hush now, we had all this out already. You promised me. . . .'

More growling; then: '. . . never a ruddy moment to ourselves!'

'There will be, there will be! Today was just unfortunate. They found a starfish. . . .'

The voices faded gradually to a mumble. Frankie hung on a bit, in case things got started again, but after a while, when even the mumbling stopped, she turned and crawled back, on all fours, to the bedroom. Jass was waiting for her, cramped into the corner between his bed and the wall, his thumb in his mouth, his eyes like soup plates.

'They've bin having a row,' said Frankie, ''bout us.' She flopped down on to her bed and picked up her starfish. 'I bet this is the only four-fingered starfish in the world. I bet if we took this to a museum they'd give us a fortune for it. But I'm not going to,' said Frankie. 'I'm going to put it in my treasure box.' She looked at Jass. 'You got a treasure box?'

Slowly, Jass shook his head.

'So where d'you keep your treasures?'

Jass took his thumb out of his mouth. 'Haven't got 'ny.'

'Haven't *got* 'ny?'

Again, he shook his head. His eyes were glued on the dead starfish.

'Have to get you some,' said Frankie. 'Tomorrow. We'll go and have look . . . get you some shells and things.' Gently she laid out her starfish on the bedside table. 'Might find a crab shell. That'd be all right, wouldn't it?'

Jass nodded.

'Right,' said Frankie. 'So that's what we'll do. We'll go and look for crab shells.'

As it happened, they couldn't go and look for crab shells because when they woke up the next day it was pouring with rain; great splattering gobbets which bounced off the rooftops and sploshed into the gutters. They spent the first part of the morning sitting in the sun room playing board games which Mrs Plastic Mac produced out of a cupboard for them. There were Fairies and Goblins, Space Walk, Big Apple and Hit the Jackpot. They played them all, one after another, and were just about to start on a second run of Big Apple when Billie Small suddenly crashed his chair back and shouted that he was sick of it. 'I didn't come all the way to Clacton to play poxy board games!'

Frankie's mum looked scared, but Frankie was secretly glad, because she hadn't come all the way to Clacton to play poxy board games, either. You could play board games at home. You came to Clacton to do other things.

Frankie's mum said, 'It's still raining out there.'

'So? A spot of poxy rain never hurt anyone!'

'But where would they go?'

'We could go on the pier,' said Frankie.

'There you are! They could go on the pier. Spend all day on the pier.'

'Thing is –' Frankie fixed him with a hard stare '– you need money.'

'Frankie Foster, you had money!'

'Spent it,' said Frankie.

There was a pause, while Frankie's mum bit her tongue and looked at Billie Small, and Billie Small set his jaw and looked at Frankie; then suddenly his cheeks exploded and he uttered a word that Hake had once uttered at school and been severely told off about.

'Take this –' he dug his hand into his trouser pocket, pulled out some coins, and thrust them at Frankie – 'and go!'

'Thank you very much,' said Frankie. She bounded across to the door, followed automatically by Jass. Jass seemed to take it for granted that wherever Frankie went, he would go too. 'What time would you like us to come back?'

'Lunch time,' said her mother.

'Tea time,' said Billie Small.

Frankie looked at the money he had given them. She didn't know whether it would last until tea time.

The pier was the most wonderful place that Frankie had ever seen. It had slot machines and Dodgem cars, and a ghost train and a slippery slope, and a hall of magic mirrors, and lots and lots of little booths selling ice cream and candy floss and funny postcards of big fat ladies paddling in the sea and tiny weedy men with their trouser legs rolled up.

Frankie bought a postcard of a rude fat lady for Hake, and a postcard of the pleasure gardens for Mr Harding (not being sure that Mr Harding would approve of rude fat ladies) and some candy floss for her and Jass, and they went down the slippery slope (on coconut mats that tickled your legs) and wandered round the hall of mirrors (but weren't allowed on the ghost train or the Dodgems without a grown-up, which was mean) and then got started on the slot machines, which was almost the bit that Frankie liked best.

'Here y'are.' She turned Jass's hand palm upwards and tipped some coins into it. 'Put that lot in your pocket and make sure no one takes it off of you . . . that's yours, that is. Do what you like with that.'

Jass stared, his face crimson.

'Well, go on!' said Frankie. 'Gotta be something here you wanna do.' She wasn't having him dogging her footsteps all round the pier, she wanted some time to herself. 'D'you want to play football? D'you want to play Space Invaders? D'you want—'

Jass found his tongue: 'Wanna go on the gwabbing machine!'

'Right. You go on the grabbing machine, I'll go on something else.'

Frankie didn't want anything as childish as a grabbing machine. What she wanted was a game of skill: a game where you had to really be with it, ready to push the right buttons and pull the right levers, like she had seen the boys that went into Foley's Fish Bar doing, at home. (Except that it wasn't home any more: she had to keep reminding herself.)

She tried three or four machines before she found Starhopper. She knew as soon as she found it that it was for her: Starhopper was a real test of skill.

First you had to get the hopper off the ground without it blowing up; then, once it was out in space, on its way to the planet Astral, you had to steer it through the swarms of meteorites that kept coming at you; then you had to do battle with the Astralites, who sent out great fleets of star warriors armed with lasers; finally, if you managed to survive all that, you had to chart your way amongst bottomless oceans and jagged mountain ranges in order to make a safe landing.

Frankie just knew that if she played it long enough she would manage to crack it. Already she had got to the stage where passers-by were stopping to watch. She could zip through the meteorites and zap the enemy starships without any trouble at all. The screen kept exploding in great firework displays of colour; mauves and reds and brightest green, rioting across the heavens as the ships went down. Zap! Pow! Vroosh! She could feel all the people sucking their breaths in with admiration. Look at that girl! Look how fast she is! Look at her reactions!

And still she couldn't quite make that last little bit. Five times she successfully negotiated blastoff, safely steered her way through the meteorites, triumphantly demolished the enemy starfleet, only to crash-land at the last minute and disappear from the screen in a shower of purple.

She had to beat it! She had to!

She tried again. Again she survived the meteorites. Again she blasted the starfleet. Again she crash-landed. . . .

This time; *this* time she would do it!

Frankie stuffed her hand into her pocket. Where was the money? The money had gone! She had run out of money! She turned, in agitation, to look for Jass, and found him standing silently at her side.

'How long you bin there?'

'Long time.'

'Got 'ny money?'

Jass shook his head.

'What, you gone and spent it all?' Trust him – one more go and she knew she'd be able to do it.

'Got this.' Jass held up a small plastic spaceman. 'Onna gwabbing machine.'

'Yeah, great.' Frankie waved it aside, impatiently. What was she supposed to do with a plastic spaceman? That wouldn't buy her another game. 'We got to get more money! Go back to the hotel and ask your dad for some.'

Jass slid his eyes away. He put the plastic spaceman into his mouth.

'Well, go on!' said Frankie. 'Quick!'

She gave him a little shove, but although he wobbled a bit and nearly fell over he still didn't make any move.

'Look, I can't go, can I?' said Frankie. 'I'm playing this machine. If I leave it, someone else'll move in. I got to stay here and guard it.'

There was a long silence; Jass stood, sucking his spaceman. Frankie could cheerfully have walloped him. Just her luck to get lumbered with a weed like that – dopey little dwarf.

A boy who had been watching her, admiring her skill, suddenly shouldered his way forward. 'Here!' He jerked his head at Frankie. 'You gonna let someone else have a go? Or you gonna hog that machine all day?'

Talk about *aggressive*. Frankie felt like smashing his face in for him.

'Fwankee . . .' Jass had taken his spaceman out of his mouth and was tugging at her. She turned, irritably.

'What?'

'I wanna go!'

'Go where?'

'*Go.*'

Frankie made an angry tutting noise. That was the trouble with seven-year olds: couldn't hold themselves. Crossly, she carted him off to the toilets (which fortunately were free, since by then she had decided that she might as well go herself) and back along the front to the Wellesley Court. The sunroom was empty, and so was the coffee lounge; they must be upstairs again. Honestly, the number of hours grown-ups spent in bed. What a waste!

Up the stairs clattered Frankie, with Jass as usual trailing at her heels. Boldly she hammered on the bedroom door. There was a moment of silence, then Billie Small's voice bellowed: 'Who's that?'

'It's us!' yelled Frankie.

More silence, then a string of dirty words; very dirty words. Mr Bagley at school had once told Hake that if ever he heard him using words like that again he would personally drag him outside by the seat of his pants and deposit him in the nearest rubbish bin.

'There's no need to be rude!' screamed Frankie. (Jass, crouched behind her in the corridor, made himself as small as he could, curled up into a little ball with his arms wrapped round her ankles. What did he think he was doing?)

The door was flung open and Billie Small stood there,

huge and immense in a white dressing gown that looked as if it had been made out of old bath towels. 'What are you kids doing back? I thought I told you to stay out till tea time?'

'We couldn't,' said Frankie, 'you didn't give us enough money.'

'You cheeky little—'

'Billie!'

'I gave those poxy kids over five quid!'

'It wasn't enough.' Frankie faced him, brazenly. 'We've spent it all. And it's still raining. *And* we're hungry.'

'Here!' Her mother suddenly appeared at the door, in her silk kimono. She pushed her purse rather nervously at Frankie. 'Take that and go and buy some fish and chips for yourselves. And just mind and keep out of trouble.'

'And this time, don't come back until you're ruddy well told to!'

The door slammed. Frankie opened her mother's purse and looked inside it. She stooped, and prodded at Jass. 'C'mon! Let's go back to the pier.'

By the end of the week, Frankie had landed safely so many times on the planet Astral that she was almost beginning to get bored with it.

5

The best thing about Worple Park was the nuthouse. The nuthouse held great fascination for Frankie. The main building was hidden behind high stone walls (who knew what went on in there?) but the grounds were wide open and spacious, with only an ordinary wooden fence dividing them from the park. If you climbed the wooden fence – which Frankie was able to do quite easily – you could hang over the top and watch what was going on.

Sometimes really funny things went on, like once when two old ladies had come by and stopped just underneath where Frankie was hanging over the fence. One old lady was wearing what looked like a woolly tea cosy on her head and the other had a pair of big green wellies, even though it was a blazing hot day. The old lady in the tea cosy had told the old lady in the wellies that she was the Queen of England and that, 'That woman who sits on the throne is just an imposter'; to which the old lady in the wellies had retorted, 'If you're the Queen of England, then I'm Margaret Thatcher!' To which the old lady in the *tea* cosy had said, 'That's right, dear . . . anything you say.'

Frankie had really enjoyed that. So had the old lady in the tea cosy. She had looked up and caught sight of Frankie and given her the most enormous, conspiratorial wink, which had made Frankie laugh so much she had nearly fallen off the fence. Billie Small had told her she was to keep away, but Frankie didn't take any notice of Billie Small. Billie Small was a creep. He was one of the worst things about Worple Park.

Another of the worst things was the flat. She had known all along that it was going to be horrid – anything belonging to Billie Small was bound to be – but she hadn't realized it was going to be quite so unspeakably foul. It was on the fifth floor of a grey concrete block specially built for the people who worked in the nuthouse. Frankie's mum said happily that it was just what she had always wanted. She said how easy it would be to keep clean, how cheap it would be to keep warm. Above all, she said, it was a place of her own.

Frankie thought that it was hideous. There wasn't any garden, and the windows didn't open properly, and the rooms were just boring square blocks, low and squat and dingy. What was more, there weren't enough of them: Frankie was still having to share with Jass.

'It isn't fair!' she wailed. 'You promised!'

'I did not,' said her mother.

'You did! You said!'

'I never did!'

It was true, when Frankie stopped to think: her mother never *had* said. Frankie had just assumed, automatically, that in a new place she would have a room of her own. Her mother had done her best. She had hung a big curtain down the middle, but still it wasn't the same. Even though she had written a large notice saying 'Private' and stuck it on Jass's side of the curtain, Frankie could still be taken by surprise at moments when she didn't want to be, like when she was looking through her treasure box or talking to her photograph of her father. (She was talking to him more and more since coming to live in this horrible place.) Not only could people walk in on her, which is what they kept doing, in spite of her notice, but they could hear her – well, Jass could hear her. He had asked her one day, in front of her mother, 'Who was that you was speaking to, Fwankie?'

'When?'

'Last night, when you was in bed . . . you was speaking to someone.'

'I was not!'

'You was,' said Jass. 'I heared you.'

'She was maybe just having a nightmare,' suggested her mother.

'Wasn't a nightmare. I heared her, she said—'

'Oh, shut *up*!' snarled Frankie.

She was furious with Jass for that. She cornered him afterwards in his bit of the bedroom and threatened to thump him if ever he listened in on her conversations again. 'Nasty little eavesdropping gnome! I'll jolly well belt you one!'

She bunched a fist, to show that she meant business. Instead of telling her to drop dead or threatening to belt her back, which was what Hake would have done, Jass shrank away from her, big-eyed and fearful. For a moment Frankie felt so irritated that she almost *wanted* to bash him; and then she felt rotten and mean. To get Hake cowering would be something, but Jass was such a weed. And he was only seven years old. It wasn't really much to boast of, beating up a seven-year old. It wasn't the sort of thing you could go round bragging about . . . 'I gave this kid a black eye. Listening in on my conversations, wasn't he? So I duffed him up one.'

'Look,' she said, 'I'll show you who I was talking to. And when I've shown you –' She wiped a finger across her throat. 'Slit your gizzard if you breathe a word!'

She took him through the curtain into her half of the bedroom, sat him on the bed and made him close his eyes while she scrabbled underneath for her treasure box.

'This is it, see?' She thrust the photograph at him. 'That's my dad, that is; my real dad. And if you ever tell anyone –' Jass started to shake again '– I shall be very

63

angry,' said Frankie. 'I won't bash you, but I'll be angry. So you got to promise ... you got to say, *I promise*—'

'Pwomise,' whispered Jass.

'That this is our secret, just between the two of us.'

'... our secwet, just atween the two of us.'

'Right!' Frankie snatched back the photograph. 'Now we're bound by an oath. That means it's you and me against the rest of them.'

She wasn't quite sure who the rest of them were, other than Billie Small, and she certainly couldn't imagine what use a trembly weed like Jass would ever be, but just for the moment there wasn't anyone else. She'd tried ringing Toenail one morning (Hake didn't have a telephone) but his mother had said that he was out playing. She'd taken Frankie's number and promised that he would call her back, but he never had, and now when Frankie rang there wasn't any reply, which probably meant they'd gone on holiday.

Usually when Toenail went on holiday he sent funny postcards, but he couldn't do that now because he didn't have Frankie's new address. Hake had it, but Hake didn't go on holiday. Nor did the Gool. Nor did Mr Harding, though that hadn't stopped him sending her a card. He'd sent one that he had chosen specially. It had a picture of a marmalade cat sitting in the middle of a flowerbed with a big fat grin on its face. (She knew that he'd chosen it specially because there had been a marmalade cat that had lived next door and quite often she and Mr Harding had enticed it over to talk to them.) There was even a special message written on the back: 'Having great difficulty doing my crosswords. Wish you were here to help me with them. My poor old brain is wearing out! Lots of luck and all my love, XXX Grandpa Harding.'

It was a lovely card, the nicest she'd ever had. It was in her treasure box now: her third best treasure, after the photograph of her father and the stamp from Jamaica. Probably if Hake had sent her one it wouldn't have been half as nice, but she still wished that he had; or that Toenail had rung. It was rotten of them not to.

'You'll make new friends quickly enough,' said her mother. 'What about the two lads over the way, now? Why don't you try playing with them?'

'Don't like them.'

'How can you say you don't like them? You don't even know them!'

Frankie didn't have to know them. She'd met them in the park; two boys of about her own age, kicking a football. Frankie enjoyed football. She had once thought of playing for Arsenal, until Hake had pointed out that Arsenal didn't have women on their teams – 'Nobody has women on their teams. They ain't strong enough.' She had bashed him for that, and Hake had bashed her back and given her a bloody nose, but at least, afterwards, he had admitted that she was a jolly sight more valuable to have on a team than the Gool or Toenail.

The boys at Worple Park hadn't even given her a chance. They'd recognized immediately that she was a girl (that was her mum's fault, that was: she'd made Frankie grow her hair for the wedding) and when she tried to join in they'd just jeered.

'Who d'you think you are? Maradona?' That had really creased them.

'Maradona!'

Ho ho ho. Ha ha ha.

'Madonna, more like!' That had creased them even more.

Frankie had stamped a foot. 'I can play football!' She mightn't be as good as Diego Maradona (who was?) but she was good. 'I was on the school team!'

'School team!' That had just about finished them off.

'Little Madonna, dancing up the wing!'

'I don't play on the wing!' Frankie had been furious: Hake and the others had never treated her like this. 'I play striker! I—'

'Look, look, I'm a Madonna!'

The bigger of the two boys, who had spiky ginger hair (Frankie *loathed* ginger hair) had crossed his hands over his chest and stood poised, like an angel (except that he looked more like a gargoyle).

'Watch out, I'm right behind yer!'

The other boy had gone charging into him. Ginger instantly dissolved into mock sobs.

'Boo hoo, you've hurted me!'

'Girls playing *football*.' The second boy had turned and given Frankie a cocky sort of grin. It wasn't hostile, exactly; but it was definitely provoking.

'You shut your fat cakehole,' Frankie said. 'Ignorant pig!'

As she had stalked off she had heard their cries echoing after her: 'You shut your fat cakehole ... ignorant pig!'

She didn't want to play football with them anyway.

For the rest of the holidays Frankie was obviously going to have to make do with Jass. He was not the ideal companion – in fact there were times when he annoyed her so much that she felt like screaming at him; but she had learnt, with Jass, that if you screamed it only made him worse. It made him even dumber, even stupider, even more dim and wet and weedy than he normally wasy. Billie Small screamed at him. He whacked him, too. He was always whacking him; every morning at six o'clock, before he left for the nuthouse, he would come into the bedroom and slap at him and pummel him. Frankie knew he did this because one morning, when she was getting sick of being woken up – who wanted to be woken up at *six o'clock?* – she crept across the room and peered through a chink at the end of the curtain to see what was going on.

She saw Jass being tipped out of bed, half asleep, and she saw Billie Small pull back the blankets and peer down at the bedclothes. Then she heard him give a grunt, tumble Jass back into bed and go off again.

This happened every morning for a week. Frankie grumbled to her mother about it: 'What's he have to keep coming in and waking everybody up for?'

But her mother either didn't know or if she did she wasn't telling. 'You just don't worry yourself about it. Take no notice and go back to sleep.'

'But what's he do it for?'

'No business of yours. Nothing to do with you.'

All very well saying nothing to do with her, but she had to sleep there, didn't she? She had to get woken up at six o'clock every morning.

'Why can't I come in with you and let him go in there if he wants to keep waking people up?'

'You can't come in with me.'

'Why can't I?'

'Because Billie and I are married, and married people sleep together! Just learn to put up with things, the same as we all have to.'

One morning Billie Small didn't go into the nuthouse because it was his day off, and on that morning they were all allowed to sleep until half-past eight. It was then that Frankie discovered the reason behind the six o'clock stripping: Jass had wet the bed. She heard a thump and a wack, and Billie Small's voice shouting, 'Do I have to get up at the crack of dawn every bloody day to stop you fouling yourself?'

She heard Jass whimpering, and then her mother's voice, from the hallway: 'Ah, now, Billie, don't be too hard on him, he's but a wee lad! He can't help it.'

'Help it? Of course he can help it! It's sheer bloody laziness!'

Frankie crawled over to her chink in the curtain. She

saw Jass standing there, shaking, holding his pyjama bottoms in one hand. She saw a grim-faced Billie Small strip the sheet from the bed and bundle both sheet and Jass out of the door. Seconds later she heard the sound of raised voices coming through the wall. She often heard raised voices through the wall. (Mr Harding had once told Frankie that he and his wife had 'hardly ever had a cross word'. Frankie's mum and Billie Small seemed to have nothing but cross words.)

Frankie picked up her dressing gown and crept off down the passage. As she passed the room next door she heard Billie Small's voice: '. . . do what I like with my own poxy child!'

In the bathroom she found a sobbing Jass standing in the bath, running cold water over himself and the sheet.

'What you doing that for?' said Frankie.

Through his sobs, Jass said that he was washing his sheet.

'In the *bath*? In cold water? There's a washing machine out there!'

'Not allowed to use the washing machine.'

'Why not?'

Jass's tears flowed afresh. 'Too dirty.'

'But that's *stupid*!' said Frankie. 'You can't wash a *sheet* in the *bath*.'

'You leave that sheet where it is!' Billie Small's bulk had appeared in the doorway. 'He soiled it, he can wash it—and I want it wrung out good and proper. I don't want no puddles on the bathroom floor. You!' He jerked his head at Frankie. 'Out!'

'But you can't w—'

'Did you hear what I said?'

'But you c—'

'OUT!'

Filled with loathing, Frankie marched from the bathroom – straight into her mother, who was on her way in.

'Frankie, wha—'

Frankie marched on.

'Fra—'

SLAM.

'Frankie Foster, will you kindly answer me when I speak to you!' The bedroom door was thrown open and her mother came storming through the curtain: 'What's all the shouting?'

'He's being foul!'

'If you're referring to Billie—'

'What's he have to go and wallop him for?'

'Because he wet the bed, that's what for!'

'So what?' The Gool had wet the bed. No one had walloped the Gool.

'So he has to be taught that it's not right!'

''Snot right to wash sheets inna *bath* . . . washing sheets inna bath's just *stupid*.'

'You don't be so cheeky!' Her mother aimed a swipe, catching Frankie round the head. 'You just keep out of what doesn't concern you! Jasper is Billie's child, it's not up to you to interfere.'

'So what about you?' screamed Frankie. 'Thought you was going to be his mum? That's what you said!'

'I may be his mum, but Billie's his dad. It's up to Billie how he disciplines him.'

'Better not try disciplining me!' yelled Frankie.

'Any more of that, my girl. . . .' Her mother drew back her arm: Frankie took a nose dive beneath the pillows. 'You just watch it, or I'll be the one that's disciplining you!'

From that point on, Billie Small had it in for her. Frankie could feel that he did from the way he glared at her, all dark and brooding out of the corners of his eyes when he thought she wasn't looking. He would like it if she wasn't

69

there. Well, and so would Frankie! Worple Park was a horrible dump. The only thing that made it bearable was hanging over the wall of the nuthouse talking to the nuts.

Some of them had become her friends, so that she didn't really think of them as nuts any more. There was a boy called Guy, with lovely dark curly hair and the brightest blue eyes that Frankie had ever seen. Guy never actually said anything (she knew his name was Guy because she had heard one of the nurses calling to him) but he would come and listen while she talked. He seemed to like Frankie talking, especially when she told him about Hake, and the gang, and the things they had done together. Once he brought her a magpie feather, which she had put in her treasure box.

Then there was a girl, whose name Frankie didn't know, who sometimes walked with her eyes on the ground, not looking at anything, and other times waved and smiled and cried 'Hi, there!'

When she did that, Frankie would always wave back and cry, 'Hi, there!' in return.

Then, of course, there was Queenie, and Mrs Thatcher. They had got in the habit, now, of walking down to the same bit of fence every morning. They knew that Frankie would be there, hanging over, waiting to talk to them. You couldn't exactly hold what Frankie would call a proper conversation. Mrs Thatcher, depending on her mood, either didn't talk at all or else she talked so much that no one could get a word in edgeways, whilst Queenie hopped from one subject to another with such bewildering rapidity that Frankie found her brain growing dizzy with the effort of trying to keep up, especially with all the interruptions which kept occurring.

The interruptions were caused by imaginary members of the public seeking audiences with the Queen, which meant that every few seconds Queenie had to keep breaking off in order to nod, very graciously, or just occasionally to bestow a knighthood or receive a bunch of flowers. (Once she had handed the flowers to Frankie to smell, and Frankie had said, 'Ooh, roses! Lovely!'

Queenie had scolded her: 'Not roses, you stupid child! Sweet peas and polyanthus.')

Frankie could never quite make up her mind whether Queenie really and truly believed that she was the Queen of England or whether she was only playing at it, like she played at Mrs Thatcher being Mrs Thatcher. Mrs Thatcher herself knew that she wasn't really Mrs Thatcher; she didn't even pretend that she was. It was Queenie who insisted that she did.

'Thinks she's Maggie Thatcher,' she would whisper to Frankie, behind her hand. 'She's mad, of course; stark mad.'

'Speak for yourself!' Mrs Thatcher would retort. 'Stupid old bag!' She wasn't as good natured as Queenie, and what was more she refused to address her as Your Majesty, which Frankie always did. Frankie didn't see that there was any harm in it. It made Queenie happy, and she didn't think the real Queen would mind – well, she might, but nobody was likely to tell her, unless Mrs Thatcher wrote her a letter out of spite. She could be spiteful, sometimes, especially when Queenie accused her of being mad and told Frankie that that was why she'd been locked up. She said that Queenie was a rat-ridden old hag and lots of other things that made Frankie's eyes pop out on stalks.

'I am not locked up, I have come here for my own protection . . . I am in hiding. There are people on the other side who are out to get me.'

Mrs Thatcher was very bothered about people being out to get her. Frankie knew the feeling. She tried to explain, without actually mentioning him by name, how Billie Small was out to get *her*, but Mrs Thatcher wasn't terribly interested in things that were happening to other people. She was very self centred. So was Queenie, but Queenie did at least have a sense of humour. She loved playing practical jokes. One morning she gave Frankie a long strip of liquorice to chew: the liquorice turned out to be a leather shoelace. Queenie laughed and laughed. (Mrs Thatcher just stood there, gazing into the distance, she had no sense of humour at all.) Another time Queenie offered Frankie a trick sweet full of pepper, which burned her throat and made her cough. Frankie had felt that that was going a bit too far, even for the Queen of England. She had told Queenie so.

'I don't think you can be Queen ... a real queen wouldn't do childish things like that!'

Queenie just gave her a little smile; sly and secretive and full of mischief. It was as if she were saying, 'Well, of course I'm not the Queen! But it's great fun, isn't it?'

One morning when Frankie was sitting astride her fence, listening to a long and rambling tale from Mrs Thatcher about how one of the nurses was out to get her (if it had been Billie Small, Frankie wouldn't have been at all surprised) when a voice that Frankie thought she recognized called, 'Hey! Your Majesty! Visitors for you.'

Queenie turned, and closed one eye at Frankie in a roguish wink. 'My loyal subjects,' she said.

'Loyal subjects!' Mrs Thatcher sniffed. 'Her brother and his wife, that's all.'

'Hey day, ladies! Who's that you're talking to?'

A figure appeared. Horrors! It was Billie Small's best mate who had been at the wedding. He stepped back a pace and peered up at the wall, shading his eyes against the sun. Frankie slid down the other side so fast she scraped her hands almost raw.

That evening, when he got home from the nuthouse, Billie Small really laid into her. He didn't bash her, he knew better than that (she'd jolly well bash him back if he did) but he roared so loud the neighbours complained. 'Didn't I tell you, to keep away? *Didn't I?* That's private property, that is! That's a hospital. Those are sick people. They're there for treatment. You do that again, I'll knock your ruddy block off!'

'I was only talking,' said Frankie.

'I don't give a monkey's what you were only doing! How many times do I have to tell you? That is PRIVATE PROPERTY. Do you know the meaning of the words private property?'

'Yes,' said Frankie. 'Can I talk to them through the gates?'

'You go anywhere near those gates, I'll have your guts for garters! This is my livelihood you're interfering with. Eleven years I've been in that job and never a foot wrong. I'm not having some poxy brat come along and jeopardize my chances. You just keep well away in future – and don't answer back! Just do as you're told, if you don't want a good thrashing.'

Her mother wasn't sympathetic in the least. 'I don't want to hear anything more about it! You've been told not to go there, so don't go there.'

'But they're my friends,' said Frankie.

'How can they be your friends? They're mad people.'

'I like mad people.'

'Don't talk so daft! They could be dangerous, for all you know.'

'They're not dangerous. They're nice. They're interesting. They—'

'Frankie, will you just shut your racket? Serve you right if he belted you one – you've been told often enough. From now on you take Jasper with you, and you keep to your own part of the park. Do I make myself clear? I don't want any more trouble!'

There wasn't anything to do in their own part of the park. The park wasn't like the Heath. There were no trees that you could climb. There were no ponds. There were no wooded areas or hilly bits. Just a scrubby patch of grass with boring concrete paths and Jass tagging along behind, wittering at her. He had become quite talkative with Frankie; too talkative, sometimes. How could you hold an intelligent conversation with a seven-year old? It was worse than Mrs Thatcher and Queenie.

One day, in desperation, for want of anything better to do, Frankie made up a story, all about a black prince who rode out of the light into the darkness and rescued a captive princess. Jass was enchanted. Next day he wanted her to tell him another one, only this time he wanted it to be about a prince who rescued a captive princess and her little brother.

'A captive princess and her faithful servant,' said Frankie. Princesses didn't have little brothers; not in any story she'd ever read. A faithful servant would come in useful for carrying all the bits and pieces of luggage, because obviously the princess would want to take certain things with her when she was rescued: treasures and things; the electric carving knife, maybe, in case they were attacked; Billie Small's leather belt with the silver buckle and the studs. They could be put in a pillow case and tied with a piece of string.

Frankie and Jass sat on one of the park benches for Frankie to tell her story. At the end of it, quite unexpectedly, the princess turned out to be another prince, in disguise, and the two princes, who were probably brothers, because princes were allowed to have brothers, rode off side by side together with their faithful servant.

'Where was they riding to?' Jass wanted to know.

'Across the world,' said Frankie.

'What was they going to do there?'

74

'Fight the foe.'

'What's foe?'

'Foe's people that are out to get you,' said Frankie. 'People like –' She stopped. People like your dad, she had been about to say. 'People like them.'

The ginger-haired boy and his mate were coming towards them along the path. The ginger-haired boy walked with a swagger, his mate, who was wearing a T-shirt with the word 'Batman' printed across it, bounced aggressively at his side. Jass slid his hand into Frankie's. 'Fwankee! Less go.'

'Go? What d'you wanna go for? I haven't finished my story yet; haven't told how they ride across the world and—'

'Eh!' The two boys had come to a halt in front of them. Ginger addressed himself to Frankie: 'Your dad works in the nuthouse, don't he? Works with the nuts.'

'That ain't my dad,' said Frankie.

'So whose dad is he?'

'His dad.' Frankie nodded at Jass, still clinging to her hand.

'So if it's his dad, what's your mum doing living with him?'

'Married to him, ain't she?'

'Oh, yeah?'

'Yeah!'

'So where's your dad?'

'Ain't here.'

'Why ain't he here?'

''Cos he's in the nick!' screeched Batman.

'No, he ain't!' screeched Frankie. 'You wash your mouth out!'

'Where is he?'

'She don't know,' said Ginger. 'I bet she never had one.'

75

'I got a dad!' said Frankie. 'Bet it's more'n you got!'

Ginger's face went a sort of mottled colour. 'You looking for trouble?'

'I'm just sitting here,' said Frankie. 'I didn't ask you to come and talk to me. Stupid dribbler.'

'You calling me names?' said Ginger.

'Yeah, I'm calling you names!'

'You just better hadn't!'

'Why? What you gonna do about it?'

'I could turn nasty,' said Ginger.

'Yeah?'

'Yeah!'

Frankie looked at him, contemptuously. 'Get stuffed, pimple face!'

'Stuff yourself, wog!'

'You say that again—' said Frankie.

Ginger said it again.

'I'll kill you for that!' screamed Frankie.

It was a passer-by who separated them. The passer-by didn't realize at first that Frankie was a girl. (She was wearing her tracksuit, and her hair had been cut again.) She hauled on Frankie's collar and shook her fiercely to and fro. 'Stop that! This instant!'

She didn't tell Ginger to stop it. Maybe that was because Ginger was the one who was coming off worse. Frankie only had a bruised wrist and a sore head: Ginger had a split lip and a bleeding nose and a nasty set of teeth marks halfway up his arm.

'You must go straight home,' said the lady, 'and get your mother to take you to the hospital. Human bites can be very nasty. As for you, you little barbarian—' She shook Frankie again, holding her by the back of her tracksuit. 'I've a good mind to take your name and address!'

'Can if you like,' said Frankie.

'Just for that,' said the lady, 'I will!' She opened her bag and pulled out a small red leather diary and a gold pencil. 'Right! Who are you and where do you live?'

'Michael Heneghan,' said Frankie, '42 Rosslyn Mansions.'

'That's a lie!' yelled Ginger. 'She lives in the flats!'

'Oh?' The lady looked more closely at Frankie. She closed her notebook with a snap. 'You know,' she said, and she sounded more reproachful, now, than angry, 'it really doesn't do any good at all to resort to violence. You only bring yourself down to their level.'

The lady walked off, leaving Frankie and Ginger at a loss. They looked at each other, united for a moment in common puzzlement; then Frankie remembered what Ginger had called her, and Ginger caught sight of the teeth marks on his arm, and they looked at each other again, and this time it was war.

'I'll get you for this!' hissed Ginger.

That evening, while Billie Small was in the kitchen eating his tea, and Jass and Frankie were in the sitting room watching television, someone rang at the door. Frankie didn't think anything about it – after all, what possible connection could it have with her? – until, suddenly, she heard loud voices, her mother's and Billie Small's, and that of an unknown woman. The unknown woman sounded shrill and angry. Frankie was just about to creep over and press her ear to the crack when Billie Small's voice, louder than the rest, shouted, 'All right, darling, you've made your point! You don't have to keep on. Just leave it to me, I'll deal with this!'

The next minute the front door was slammed shut, the sitting-room door thudded back against the wall, and Billie Small was there, bare chested with his trousers hanging down beneath his gut and horrible black hairs growing all over him. 'Right, you little so and so!' Huge and threatening, he advanced upon Frankie. Grabbing her by the ear, he yanked her out of her chair. 'I've just about had a bellyful of you! Nothing but bloody trouble from the word go!'

'What made you do it, Frankie?' Her mother stood a few paces inside the door. '*Biting* someone – that's no sort of a way to carry on!'

'You're dead right it isn't!' Billie Small dragged her towards him. 'Bit of old-fashioned discipline is what you need, my girl! If I had my way, I'd thrash the living daylights out of you!'

Frankie faced him, defiantly; as defiantly as she could, being held by one ear. 'Wasn't my fault!'

'Wasn't your fault? What do you mean, it wasn't your fault? Wasn't your fault you flew at the kid and clawed him half to death? Wasn't your fault you sunk your teeth into his arm? Wasn't your fault you damn near broke his nose? That boy's had to be taken to the casualty and be given injections. If he goes down with something, it'll be entirely due to you! And then you stand there and have the brass face to tell me it wasn't your fault?'

'I just don't see how you can say that, Frankie! You were the one that started it – he's a witness to prove it. Just tore into him, he said; tore into him, for no reason. He'll stand up in court and testify.'

'Well, come on! Don't stand there dumb! What's the excuse?'

'He called me something.'

'Called you what?'

She wasn't saying what; wild horses wouldn't drag it out of her.

'*Called you what*?'

'Whatever it was,' said her mother, 'you'll have brought it on yourself.'

Frankie was indignant: 'I never!'

'You and that tongue of yours . . . I know you! You'll have asked for it.'

'*I never!*'

'It's always you that starts these things. Always the same. Always—'

'I DIDN'T EFFING START IT!'

'You—!' Billie Small took a swipe at her. Frankie ducked; she was expert at ducking. 'You come into my house using that kind of language . . . I'll ruddy murder you!'

'Billie! For God's sake!' cried Frankie's mum.

'You just keep out of it! I've listened to you long enough. It's about time this brat had some discipline knocked into her!'

Billie Small pulled back his arm, fist clenched ready to smash. Suddenly, before the blow could fall, Jass had raced across the room and was clutching Frankie round the legs.

'Stop it, stop it. Don't hit her! Don't hit her!'

'You get out of it, you poxy little creep!'

Jass was jerked to his feet and sent hurtling back against the wall. He screamed, in terror.

'And you can stop that racket if you don't want a clip round the ear!'

Jass subsided, whimpering.

'Why pick on him?' shouted Frankie. 'What's he done?'

'Frankie, for the love of God,' whispered her mother.

Billie Small swung round. He was breathing, heavily, his bare chest heaving. Frankie knew that for two pins he would belt her one. They stood there, facing each other. 'I've only got one thing to say to you, my girl.' Slowly, menacingly, Billie Small jabbed at Frankie with a finger, pushing her backwards. 'You just watch it. If you want to stay healthy . . . you just watch it!'

Later that evening, when Billie Small had gone down to the pub and Jass was in bed, Frankie's mum said, 'Why do you have to do it to me, Frankie? All the time, upsetting him . . . as if I don't have enough to put up with!'

'Wasn't my fault,' said Frankie.

'Don't start on that again! Of course it was your fault. It's always your fault. You push him into it. He's not a violent man. If you could just be nice to him . . . for the Lord's sake, Frankie! I don't want to see you get hurt; you're all I've got. But you must understand – look at it from my point of view. How do you think I feel? Stuck between the two of you? What am I supposed to do? We've all got to live together.'

'Why?' said Frankie.

'Because we're a family is why! Or at least, we're supposed to be.' Frankie's mum sniffed and wiped the back of her sleeve across her nose. 'You can go to bed now, I've had enough of you.'

'I can't go to bed now, it's only eight o'clock!'

'I don't care! Just do as you're told.'

'But it's—'

'GO TO YOUR BED WHEN I TELL YOU!'

It wasn't fair. It just wasn't *fair*. She hated this place. She hated Billie Small. She hated her mother. Serve her right if she ran away.

Why shouldn't she run away? Other people did. You read about it all the time. People running away from home.

There was just one problem: where could she run to?

'Fwankee?' Jass's voice came quavering at her from the other side of the curtain.

'It's all right,' said Frankie. 'He's gone out.'

'Fwa—'

'It's *all right*,' said Frankie.

She knew where they could run to.

6

'Mr Harding's my granddad,' said Frankie.

'Man inna picture,' said Jass.

'*No*. That's my dad.'

'Go to your dad.'

'Can't go to my dad: my dad's in Jamaica.'

'Where J'maica?'

'Miles away. Other side of the world.'

'Where the princes went an' the faithful servant?'

'Right.'

Jass thought about it. 'Go to J'maica,' he said.

'Haven't got the money. Costs a lot of money, go to J'maica.' She had only just had enough to pay their tube fares from Worple Park to Hampstead. She didn't have anything left for taking them back, but that didn't matter: Frankie had no intention of ever going back. When Mr Harding heard how hateful it was at Worple Park, and the way Billie Small carried on, flying out at everyone, belting them and bawling at them, he was bound to say they could stay there with him, in Beechcroft Road. He had dozens of empty rooms, he wouldn't mind Jass and Frankie having two of them. (One for Frankie, one for Jass: this time she really was going to have a room of her own.)

'Mr Harding's got a garden,' she said. She took Jass by the hand as they stepped out into the road. 'A garden you can play in . . . trees you can climb.'

Then there was the Heath, and Hake and the Gool and Toenail. How surprised they would be when she turned up! This evening, when she had put Jass to bed, she would go round and visit Hake; tell him she was back. She bet he'd be pleased to see her, he must be getting really bored with Toenail on holiday and only the Gool for company. The Gool was all right in a gang, but he wasn't much use by himself. And Hake and Frankie had always been best mates.

Frankie gave a little skip. It was going to be fun, living with Mr Harding! She and Jass could have the attic rooms, right at the top. Mr Harding was always saying how the attic rooms were wasted because no one ever went up there.

'And we won't be any nuisance,' said Frankie. 'We'll get our own meals and stuff. Just get things we like, like crisps and choc'late bars. Things that don't need cooking. We don't want to do no cooking; cooking's boring. And when it's winter we can get stuff like fish 'n chips, an' hamburgers.'

Wonderful visions rose before her. They would never have to eat things they didn't like (except, perhaps, occasionally at school). They would never have to do any washing up – they could eat straight out of the tin (or the paper if it was fish and chips) and drink from the can, and use fingers instead of knives and forks. Who needed knives and forks? Who needed half the things that grown-ups got so bothered about? Plates and dishes, and cups and saucers: tablecloths and dusters and drying-up cloths and soap powder. It was all clutter. She and Jass wouldn't have any of it, up in their attics.

Frankie humped her pillowcase over her shoulder. It clinked as she walked, and was quite heavy. Inside was her treasure box, three pairs of clean pants – one pair for her, two pairs for Jass, in case he had an accident – the electric carving knife, Billie Small's belt with the silver studs, a tube of toothpaste and a teddy bear.

Frankie had included the toothpaste at the last moment,

because if you didn't clean your teeth they got all holes in them and then you had to go to the dentist, and if there was one thing Frankie hated it was going to the dentist. (He always said, 'Be a big brave girl, it'll all be over in a second.' It never was over in a second, and she didn't want to be a big brave girl.)

The teddy bear belonged to Jass. It was horrid and smelly because it slept with him at night, and Frankie was pretty sure that he'd weed over it, but he wouldn't go anywhere without it. The carving knife she had taken from the drawer in the kitchen while her mother was vacuuming in another room, and Billie Small's belt she had removed from a pair of trousers left hanging over a chair. She had taken the carving knife in case they ran into muggers on the tube. She didn't quite know why she had taken the belt, except that she had always wanted it; and since Billie Small was now going to be rid of her, which was what he had always wanted, she didn't really see that he could complain. It was a fair exchange; sort of.

'Fwankee!' Jass was tugging at her hand.

'What?'

'I want to go!'

'You can go when we get to Mr Harding's.'

'Want to go *now*.'

'Well, you can't; there isn't anywhere. Besides, we'll be there in a minute, it's only just down the road. 'Member? When you come before?' Jass looked at her, doubtfully. 'When you come to tea with us – when you come to the *wedding*. 'Member?'

Jass nodded and said, 'Mm,' but he didn't seem too certain.

'Just down here,' said Frankie. 'Round the corner . . . and we're there!'

It was Mrs Gedge who opened the door. Frankie had forgotten how horrible she was.

'Oh,' she said, when she saw Frankie. 'It's you.'

'We've come to see Mr Harding,' said Frankie.

'I'm afraid you can't see Mr Harding. Mr Harding's not well.' There was a pause, then she added: 'I'm sorry.'

She wasn't sorry. Frankie bet she wasn't one bit sorry.

'All that journey for nothing,' said Mrs Gedge. She stood holding the door, obviously expecting Frankie to go. Frankie stood there, stubbornly. She wasn't sure that she believed it, Mr Harding being ill; he had never been ill before. Her eyes switched from Mrs Gedge to the hallway beyond. Mr Harding's stick was in the hall stand, which certainly meant that he was indoors. (He couldn't even walk across the garden without his stick, his legs were too wobbly.) The big clock at the end of the hall said half-past three. He would be dozing in his armchair in the back room, that was where he would be! Mr Harding always had a doze in the afternoon. He sat down to do his crossword and he just dozed off.

For a wild moment Frankie thought of diving past Mrs Gedge and shrieking, 'Mr Harding, I'm here!' but before she could do so Jass had started plucking urgently at the leg of her tracksuit. She suddenly remembered that he wanted to go. Mrs Gedge, looking down at him, said, 'Such a pity. You should have telephoned.'

She made as if to close the door. Frankie, instantly, wedged her foot in it. 'Jass wants the toilet.'

There was the downstairs toilet, at the end of the hall; the one they had used after the wedding, when they had all come back for the knees-up. To get to the downstairs toilet you had to go past the door of the back room, where Mr Harding was. 'He'll wet himself if he doesn't go.'

Mrs Gedge pursed her lips. 'You'd better come through.'

She didn't want them to go through; Frankie could tell. Frankie was an expert at knowing when people didn't want her.

84

The door of the back room was closed. As they walked past it Frankie shouted, 'Ha! Ha ha!' in as loud a voice as she possibly could. It was a silly sort of thing to shout, but at least it would let Mr Harding know that she was there. Mrs Gedge hissed at her angrily. 'Do you mind not making that noise? There's a sick man in the house!'

She needn't think Frankie believed *that*.

While Jass was using the toilet, Mrs Gedge stood guard outside. That was to prevent Frankie from going back and waking Mr Harding. He was obviously in one of his extra deep dozes, dreaming about his wife. (He had told Frankie once that that was what he liked best about being asleep: 'I see her again,' he had said.)

When she went back up the passage she would shout even louder than before. She would shout, 'Hi, Mr Harding, I'm here!' Mrs Gedge could turn round and wallop her if she liked. She didn't care.

'Why, might one ask,' said Mrs Gedge, 'are you carrying a pillowcase around with you?' Her lips drew back over her teeth in something that faintly resembled a smile (or a vampire about to sink its fangs). 'Have you got the family silver in there?'

Before Frankie could think up a suitable reply, there was a knock at the front door. 'Excuse me,' said Mrs Gedge, 'that'll be the doctor.'

It *was* the doctor. It was Dr Robbins that Frankie had had when she had broken her arm. He saw Frankie and waved and said, 'Hello, there! How are you?'

'I'm all right,' said Frankie.

'No more broken bones?'

Frankie shook her head.

'Good! That's what I like to hear.'

Frankie watched as Dr Robbins disappeared up the stairs with Mrs Gedge. She didn't bother going and looking in the back room to see if Mr Harding were there. She knew, now, that he wouldn't be.

Jass came out of the toilet. 'Fwankee, let's go!'

Go where? There wasn't anywhere they *could* go. She wasn't going back to Worple Park. She wasn't ever going back to Worple Park.

'So there we are,' said Mrs Gedge, coming back down the stairs. 'I'm afraid that's it.' She opened the front door. 'Give my regards to your mother. Tell her, by the way, that I had to get a man in to see to that washing machine. The filter was jammed; I don't know what she'd been doing with it. Also, we seem to be short on kitchen cutlery. And bed linen.' Her eye fell on Frankie's pillow-case, tied at the neck with its piece of string. The pillowcase clinked as Frankie walked past. 'I suppose your mother does know that you're here?' said Mrs Gedge.

'Yes,' said Frankie.

'It seems a long way for her to let you come, all by your-selves. Still –' Mrs Gedge hunched a shoulder. 'Some people don't seem to care what their offspring get up to.'

'We wanted to see Mr Harding,' said Frankie.

'Mr Harding is very ill. He wouldn't be able to talk to you even if you did see him.'

'He's not going to die, is he?' said Frankie.

'I'm afraid I can't tell you that,' said Mrs Gedge. 'Perhaps if you'd care to ring up, or get your mother to ring up—'

Frankie stood, clutching at her pillowcase. 'It's just that he promised me.'

'Promised you what?'

'He promised me, when he died . . . he said I could have his silver pencil.'

Mrs Gedge looked down at Frankie with distaste. 'What a nasty, grabbing, evil-minded child you are!'

Frankie was indignant. She wasn't nasty and grabbing! Mr Harding had *promised*. She bet that horrible fat Donna had her eye on it, that was what it was. Old Fatso wanted her pencil.

Brooding darkly, Frankie slouched up the road, Jass trailing at her side.

'Fwankee—'

'What?'

'We going home now, Fwankee?'

'Going home?' She rounded on him, fiercely. 'How can we go home? We've run away! I told you, we're not *going* home.' She had left a note for her mother, propped on the kitchen table. WE ARE LEAVING HOME. WE ARE GOING TO LIVE SOMEWHERE ELSE. How could they go home after that?

'Where we going to go, Fwankee?'

Frankie knitted her brows together in a scowl. 'Dunno.' Anywhere but Worple Park, that was all she knew.

They walked on, down Beechcroft Road, round the corner, into the High Street. Hake lived near the High Street – well, quite near. They could always go and see Hake.

'Fwankee—' Jass's voice came quavering at her.

'*What?*'

'I'm hungwy!'

Frankie was starting to grow pretty hungry, too. All there had been for lunch was a measly tin of baked beans, because that was all there was in the cupboard. Her mother had promised them 'something nice' when she came back from the shops; but it was while she was away at the shops that Frankie and Jass had left home.

'I know what we'll do,' said Frankie. 'We'll go and see my friend.'

They bumped into Hake halfway along the High Street. He was coming towards them with a boy called Kevin Parsons. Kevin Parsons had been one of Frankie's greatest enemies at school. Frankie had once clawed him for calling her a cow, and after that Kevin Parsons had said she wasn't just a cow, but a spiteful cow, and threatened to work her over. Hake had said that if ever he did he would have the gang to reckon with. Now here he was, walking down the High Street with him.

Frankie stood glowering, waiting for Hake to notice her. For a minute she almost thought he wasn't going to, then he stopped and said, 'Hi, Frankie!'

Frankie said, 'Where you off to?'

'Going round Kev's place. What you doing here?'

'I've run away,' said Frankie.

'Yeah?'

'Yeah.'

There was a silence.

'What you done that for?' said Kevin.

'Didn't like it.'

'What, where you was?'

'Worple Park. It's horrible.'

'So where you gonna go?'

'Dunno yet.'

They stood, looking at her.

'Crazy,' said Kevin.

Frankie bristled. 'What is?'

'You,' said Kevin.

'Don't see what's crazy about it.'

'Running off . . . it's crazy!'

'I run off once,' said Hake. 'Went up the Heath. Stayed away all day.'

Frankie tossed her head. 'I'm not just staying away all day! I'm staying away f'r ever.'

''S what you think,' said Kevin.

''S what I know,' said Frankie.

'Nah.' Kevin shook his head. 'They'll get yer. Send Old Bill after yer. That's what they do.'

'Won't know where to find me, will they? Not less someone tells 'em.'

'I won't tell 'em,' said Hake.

There was a pause. Frankie looked at Kevin.

'I won't tell 'em . . . but they'll still get yer!'

'Better not try,' said Frankie. She tapped at her pillowcase. 'I got a secret weapon in here.'

'What kind of secret weapon?'

''Lectric knife.'

''Lectric knife?'

'Yeah. Switch it on, it 'lectrocutes people. That's what I'll do, anyone tries to get me . . . I'll 'lectrocute 'em.'

'You could get put away for doing that,' said Kevin.

'Think I care?'

Another silence fell. Jass tugged at Frankie's hand. 'Fwa—'

'Shuddup!' said Frankie.

Hake shifted, uneasily. 'Best get going now. Got to get round to Kev's place.'

'Yeah, got things to do,' said Kev.

'See ya.'

Frankie watched as they walked away. 'Got 'ny money?' she called.

They stopped, and exchanged glances. 'I ain't,' said Kev.

Hake dug a hand into the pocket of his jeans. 'Seventy p's all I got.'

'C'n I have a lend of it?'

Hake hesitated. 'You c'n have a lend of fifty.' A bit shamefaced, he counted out fifty pence. ''s all I got, see, to last me. She ain't givin' me none this week. Said I ain't done nothing to deserve it.'

'I'll give it you back,' said Frankie. 'Honest.'

'If they ain't put you inside,' said Kev.

'Drop dead!' said Frankie.

No one was putting *her* inside. They'd have to catch her first. She slung her pillowcase back over her shoulder. As she did so, the electric carving knife chinked comfortingly against the studs on Billie Small's belt. Just as well she'd brought it. . . .

They spent Hake's fifty pence on bars of chocolate and walked up to the Heath to eat them. When they'd eaten them, Jass said: 'What we going to do next, Fwankee?'

'I'm thinking,' said Frankie.

'What we going to—'

'I'm *thinking*,' said Frankie.

Hake had said that when he ran away he had spent all day on the Heath. Frankie couldn't see any reason why she and Jass shouldn't spend all night on the Heath. Lots of people slept in the open. Gypsies, tramps. She had seen tramps; they slept in cardboard boxes.

'We going to play something, Fwankee?'

'No!' What did he think this was: a game? They were *running away*. It was very serious. 'Just shut up,' said Frankie, 'and let me think.'

She didn't know where you got cardboard boxes from. She had never seen anyone selling them, and even if they did, she hadn't any money. Perhaps you only needed a cardboard box if it was cold. It wasn't cold now, it was as warm as toast. Last night in the flat it had been so unbearable that Frankie had had to kick all the bedclothes off. That settled it: they would sleep on the Heath. Frankie jumped up. 'Let's go!'

'Where we going to, Fwankee?'

'Going to find a place to sleep.'

It took a long time to find a suitable spot, but they found one at last, in the middle of a clump of gorse bushes. 'This'll do,' said Frankie. She dumped her pillowcase on the ground, glad to be rid of its weight. Both her shoulders had grown quite sore. 'Make a nice bedroom, this will.'

Jass's eyes grew big. 'Going to sleep *here*?'

'Why not?' said Frankie.

Jass looked round at the gorse bushes; his lip began to quiver.

'We can pretend we're gypsies,' said Frankie. 'It'll be fun.'

Just because it was going to be fun didn't mean they

90

could go to bed dirty, or without cleaning their teeth, so after sweeping the bedroom floor, clearing away all the odd prickly bits of gorse and a couple of old Coca Cola cans, Frankie took their toothbrushes and her photograph of her father out of the pillowcase and led the way across the Heath to the fountain. As they went she laid a trail of broken twigs and scraps of chocolate wrapping so they could be sure of finding their way back. She had once read in a story about two children doing this. The children had laid a trail by unpicking their hand-knitted jumpers and using the wool like a ball of string, but Frankie didn't have a hand-knitted jumper, and neither did Jass. She reckoned broken twigs would do just as well.

'And then, you see, in the morning, if you want a fire, you can c'llect them up and use them for firewood.'

'We not going to be here inna *morning*?' said Jass.

'Course we are!' said Frankie. 'Where d'you think we're going to be?'

Jass put his thumb in his mouth and didn't say anything.

After they had cleaned their teeth at the fountain, and washed their hands and faces, and followed the trail of broken twigs back to their bedroom in the gorse bushes, there didn't seem very much else left to do except go to bed. It was a bit earlier than usual – in fact it was quite a lot earlier than usual, it was earlier even than Jass's normal bedtime – but as Frankie said, 'You get tired, being out in the air. And we'll want to be up early tomorrow.'

They lay down and closed their eyes. Jass was cuddling his teddy bear. A few minutes passed, then he said: 'Fwankee. . . .'

'What?'

'I can't get to sleep!'

'Try.'

A few more minutes, then: 'You still 'wake, Fwankee?'

'Mm.'

'I'm still 'wake.'

'Count sheep,' said Frankie.

Jass, obedient, started counting: 'One – two – fwee –'

'Not out *loud*!' said Frankie.

More minutes passed. Lots of minutes passed. It was still daylight. Birds were still twittering, bees were still buzzing, ants and beatles still scurried through the grass. Frankie turned over on to her stomach.

'I've counted nearly fwee hundwed,' said Jass.

'Got to count more'n three hundred.'

'How many I got to count?'

'Got to count . . . five thousand.'

'Five *fousand*?'

'Five thousand and one.'

'Then will I be asleep?'

'Yes,' said Frankie. 'Then you'll be asleep.'

Jass sighed, deeply. For a while there was silence. Frankie watched an ant in the grass, carrying another ant. She wondered if there were snakes. The Gool had claimed, once, to have seen an adder, but you couldn't really rely on the Gool; it had probably just been a worm. Frankie wouldn't mind seeing a snake. She had asked, last Christmas, when her mother had said she couldn't have a cat or a dog because they were too much trouble, whether she could have a python. If she had a python it could coil on her bed at night, and loop itself round the clothesline and hang around on the tops of doors. A python wouldn't be any trouble. She'd discussed it with Mr Harding and he'd agreed that a python would be interesting, he'd just doubted whether you could cuddle it like you could a furry thing. He'd suggested perhaps a gerbil, or a hamster. But then Frankie's mum—

'Fwankee!'

'What?'

'I've counted five fousand.'

92

'You can't've done!' She bet he didn't even *know* up to five thousand.

'I have,' said Jass. 'And I'm still awake.'

This time, it was Frankie who sighed. 'Want me to tell you a story?'

'Yes!' Jass bounced up, immediately. 'Tell a story!'

'All right.' Frankie rolled over on to her back. 'Once upon a time . . .'

Once upon a time there were two children called Jass and Frankie who ran away from home and hid on the Heath, and some mean and beastly pig went and told the police and the police came and nabbed them, bursting into their bedroom in the gorse bushes and surrounding them on all sides before Frankie ever got a chance to zap them with her electric carving knife.

Frankie was furious. She thought at first that it must have been Kevin Parsons shooting his mouth off, because otherwise how would the police have known where to look? How could they possibly have guessed that she would be up on the Heath? It was only later – ages later, when she had already worked out several ways of getting her revenge – that she discovered it hadn't been Kevin Parsons at all, but Mrs Gedge.

Frankie had tried telling the police that she didn't want to go home, that she was quite happy living all by herself in the middle of her gorse bushes, but the police had just laughed, as if it were a joke, and the policewoman who was there had said, 'And what about your poor mum? Dead worried, she must be!'

Frankie didn't reckon her mum had been worried at all. First thing she said, as she opened the front door and saw Frankie and Jass and the policewoman, was, 'Oh! So you're back, are you? I thought you wouldn't have gone far.'

93

The second thing she said, when the door had been closed and the policewoman had gone back downstairs, was: 'Causing all this trouble for everyone! Getting yourselves brought home in a police car. Oh my God, Frankie!' She suddenly crushed Frankie against her, almost cracking her head open against her ribcage. 'I've been having nightmares about you! The things you read in the newspapers—' She stopped. 'What in heaven's name have you got in that pillowcase?'

The pillowcase was yanked away from Frankie and upended on the kitchen table before she could do anything to stop it. Out fell the teddy bear, out fell the three pairs of pants, out fell the electric carving knife and Billie Small's belt and Frankie's treasure box.

'Frankie Foster!' Her mother snatched at the carving knife and the belt. 'I never thought I'd live to see the day! Running away is one thing, but *stealing*! For God's sake, Frankie! That's terrible!'

7

'Once upon a time –' Frankie settled herself into a comfortable position, cross-legged, on the bed. 'Once upon a time, there were two children. The children were called –'

She paused. Jass, kneeling at the foot of the bed, wriggled in anticipation. 'The children were called ... Cuthbert and Edwina!' Jass's face puckered, uncertainly. 'That's what they were called on their birth certificates,' said Frankie, relenting. 'But in everyday life they were called—'

'Jass an' Fwankee!'

'Jass and Frankie. Jass was seven years old—'

'Nine!' said Jass. Jass had a thing about being nine. He seemed to think that when he was nine he would be grown up and could do what he liked.

'All right,' said Frankie. 'Jass was nine, and Frankie was twelve.' If Jass could add a couple of years, then so could she. 'Frankie was the leader. Jass did whatever Frankie said.' Jass nodded. 'Sometimes Frankie said, "Put your right hand up!!" ' Jass, obedient, stuck up his right hand. 'Or, "Pull a funny face!" ' Jass pulled one. ' "Go cross-eyed ... stick your tongue out ... push your nose up." ' Frankie shrieked. 'You look ridiculous!'

After Jass had looked at himself in the mirror looking ridiculous, and Frankie had said that he looked like a pig, and then Frankie had tried looking like a pig, and then they had both tried looking like a whole succession of animals – frogs and toads and elephants and mice (Jass made an excellent mouse: Frankie was better at frogs) – after all that, they went back to the story.

'The two children lived in a flat in a 'normous tower block. It was the biggest tower block in the whole world, it was a hundred'n eight floors high and it didn't have any lifts, so you had to walk all the way up and all the way down, and it took a whole day to walk down and nearly a whole week to walk up. Sometimes as they walked up people c'llapsed and died, it was so erzausting. Other times they starved nigh unto death on account of not carrying 'nuff food with 'em. The flat the children lived in was horrible. It was all dark and mouldy, with big mushrooms growing on the floor and black squelchy stuff all dribbling off the walls.'

'Ugh!' Jass shuddered.

'It was evil,' said Frankie. 'And the children's parents was evil, an' all. The parents was *horrible*.'

'Say what they did! Say what they did!'

'They kept the children locked up in a cupboard.'

'And they beated them!'

'And they beat them, and starved them, and when it was time for bed they hung them upside down from hooks in the ceiling.'

'And the food what they give them! Tell about the food!'

'The food was all poisoned,' said Frankie. 'There was maggotty stew –'

'Eeugh!'

'– and cups of cold sick –'

'*Eeugh!*'

'– and scum-and-matter pie with huge great scabs 'stead of pastry.'

'EEUGH!'

'And the children got so hungry –'

'– they had to pick their noses!' Jass rolled over on to his back, squealing and kicking his legs in the air.

'Yes, and it made them ill,' said Frankie. She said this just in case Jass should start getting ideas: he was always sticking his fingers up his nose. 'You know what happens, don't you?' she said. 'Know what happens if you pick your nose too much?'

Jass stopped squealing. He looked at her, doubtfully.

'Your head caves in,' said Frankie, 'and all your brains drop out . . . that was what the parents was doing it for, keeping them starved; they was waiting for them to pick their noses till their heads caved in so's the parents could dig their brains out and eat them. That was what they was after all the time – their brains. They was going to make a special brain stew and invite their friends round for a party.'

The brains were a new touch: Jass hadn't heard this bit before. He sat up, anxiously. 'Tell how they wan away!'

'One day,' said Frankie, 'the children packed all their b'longings into a piller case and crept out at dead of night, down the fire escape . . . down – and down – and down – and down . . . till by the time they reached the bottom it was morning and it was getting light.'

'And they 'scaped!'

'Not yet,' said Frankie. There was a long way to go yet. She had to tell how they found themselves all shut in by barbed wire and electric fencing, and how the wicked parents came after them, and how at the last minute Frankie had a brilliant idea and pulled out the electric carving knife and slashed at the fence with it, and the carving knife blew all the fuses – POW! – so that the electricity went off.

Frankie knew about blowing fuses. Last week, knocking a nail into the bedroom wall (to hang up her photograph of Maradona that she had cut out of the newspaper) she had fused all the lights. *And* the television. Billie Small had been down at the pub at the time. Frankie's mum had come running into the bedroom, shouting to know what was going on. 'Oh, my God, Frankie!' When she had seen the nail sticking out of the wall, her face had turned white as a sheet, so that all her freckles stood out like big brown blobs. 'Oh, my God, you've done it this time! He'll kill you for sure!'

Billie Small hadn't killed her, but he had shaken her, and bawled at her, and smashed her against the door, and smacked her ears until her head was ringing. Frankie had borne it all in silence. She wouldn't give him the satisfaction of crying; not even if he beat her to a pulp.

He hadn't quite beaten her to a pulp, though very nearly – all her bones, afterwards, had felt like jelly, and she was sure her brains had come loose and were rattling about inside her head. Frankie hadn't shed a single tear. It was her mother who had cried. She had said, 'Why do you have to keep *doing* these things? He'd be all right if you just didn't keep upsetting him! Why, for God's sake, can't you just *behave yourself*?'

Frankie had lain rigid in bed, with her aching ribs and throbbing ears and her bones that had gone all to jelly, with her brains rattling about inside her head. It wasn't any use trying to defend herself. All she'd wanted to do was hang her photograph of Maradona on the wall. She'd cut it all neatly and stuck it on a piece of card taken from a cereal box and bound it with the special blue insulating tape that Billie Small kept in the kitchen cupboard, and even made a little loop on the back, out of cotton. It had looked ever so good; almost professional. She'd just wanted it on the wall by her bed, where she could see it when she was lying down. She hadn't known they kept electric wires hidden behind there. Her mother seemed to think she'd done it on purpose. She said that even if Frankie hadn't known about the wires she should have had more sense than to go knocking nails in. She didn't even have her photograph of Maradona any more because Billie Small had seized on it in his rage and torn it up. When he'd seen the blue insulating tape he'd grown madder than ever and really fetched Frankie a thump.

'You know where you'll end up, don't you? Behind bars, that's where!' He'd accused her of being a vandal and a thief. (He hadn't known about her having pinched his belt: her mother had kept that from him.) He said if there was any more of it he'd have her up before the courts and get her put away.

'He could, you know, Frankie.' Her mother had stood by the bed, wringing her hands and sounding tearful. 'The things you've done just recently ... and not even his child! He didn't have to take you in – there's many men as wouldn't. And this is the way you repay him! You'd just better watch your step from now on or you'll find yourself in care. And it won't be any use looking to me! I won't be able to help you. God knows, I've done as much as I can. I've just about reached the end of my tether.'

Afterwards, in the darkness, Jass had crept into Frankie's half of the bedroom and whispered, 'Wun away, Fwankee?' She had gritted teeth and said, 'Yeah – and next time it'll be for real!'

She'd only said it to keep Jass happy. Running away wasn't any use; not without someone to run to. Frankie had thought and thought but she couldn't think of one single person who would be pleased to see her. Hake wouldn't, now that he was going round with her arch enemy. Kevin Parsons hated her, and she hated Kevin Parsons. And anyway, she still owed Hake fifty pence. (Billie Small had stopped her pocket money until further notice to teach her a lesson.)

Olive wouldn't want her, she thought Frankie was nothing but trouble, she had been saying so for years. 'That girl is nothing but trouble. You mark my words – if her father was bad news, she's even worse!'

The lady in the sweetshop had had a soft spot for her. She had said that Frankie was a bright spark and a goer; but the lady in the sweet shop had a husband who was out of work and a son who lived in a wheelchair and had to be washed and fed like a baby and was going to die before he was twenty-one. Frankie's mum always said that how that woman coped, she just didn't know.

The morning after Billie Small had thumped her, when Frankie would have liked to kill him, she had seriously considered going to the lady in the sweetshop and asking if she could live with her – because after all, when her son died she would probably want another child – but then there was the problem of Jass. She couldn't see the lady in the sweetshop wanting him as well. Frankie could make herself useful, serving sweets and stacking shelves, but Jass was too young and too daft. Mr Harding was the only person who might have wanted him, but Mr Harding was so ill that he had had to be taken to the hospital. Frankie knew this because her mother had rung Mrs Gedge to thank her for telling the police about Frankie (and to have words with her about the washing machine and the missing cutlery and bedclothes). Mrs Gedge had said that nobody knew whether Mr Harding was ever going to come home again. Frankie hadn't liked to ask about her silver pencil.

'Fwankee!' Jass leaned forward on the bed and dabbed at her, impatiently. 'Make it happen!'

He wanted her to go on with the story: he wanted to get to the bit where they escaped. Frankie forced herself to continue. 'They reach the barbed wire and frantically they rush up and down, looking for a way to get out. But there isn't any way! The children is trapped! And behind them comes their parents, running and shouting, and all the people what live in the block start running, and they're all chasing them, they're all trying to get them, and they turn

100

and run in the opposite direction, and this time they come
to a 'lectric fence.'

''lectric fence!' This was the bit that Jass liked.

'And they know, if they touch it, they'll be dead.'

Jass crept closer. There was a pause.

'And evwybody's catching up on them,' prompted Jass.
He knew it off by heart.

'Everybody's catching up on them, and their parents is
right behind, breathing down their necks like evil
dragons—'

'And they take out the 'lectwic knife—'

'They take out the 'lectric knife—' Jass wriggled,
excitedly. He always grew excited at this point. He
couldn't wait to get to the bit where the fence went up in a
cloud of smoke and the children escaped. 'They take out
the 'lectric knife,' said Frankie, 'but before they can use
it—'

Before they could use it? Jass's eyes went big. He licked
his lips, apprehensively.

'Before they can use it,' said Frankie, 'their parents has
jumped on them!' It wasn't any use thinking you could
escape; she'd tried escaping. What they needed was someone to come and rescue them. ' "You hateful little
fiends!" cries the father. "I am going to bash you! I am
going to smash you and hash you and mash you to a pulp!" '

Jass swallowed.

' "Take them back upstairs," cries the mother, "and
lock them up. I have made a nice vomit pudding with
grollies on top. They can have that for their supper. They
will eat it if I have to force it down them. This will be
their punishment."

' "No, no!" roars the father, "I want blood! I am going
to beat them!"

' "I cannot stop you," says the mother. "If you want to
b—" '

101

Frankie broke off.

'Telephone!'

In one bound she was across the bedroom, crouching at the door. Frankie always believed in knowing what was going on; she always listened in to telephone conversations. She lived in hope that one day it would be someone from the nuthouse saying that one of the nuts had strangled Billie Small. She would, if she were a nut. If she were big enough. Beautiful Guy had been big enough, but Guy wasn't into violence. Frankie had once watched Guy remove snails from the path and put them on the garden so they wouldn't be crushed. (She always did the same, now, whenever she noticed a snail that might be in danger.)

With one ear pressed to the crack, Frankie heard her mother pick up the receiver and say 'Yes?' Frankie's mum always answered the telephone as if she expected there to be someone at the other end waiting to say nasty things to her. Perhaps this time there was, for the next thing she said, in tones of sharp suspicion, was: 'Who is that?'

Frankie perked up. The nuthouse?

'I thought I recognized that voice. How did you know where to find me?'

Not the nuthouse. Her mother wouldn't ask the nuthouse how they knew where to find her. Frankie drooped again, but went on listening; after all, you never knew. He could have been run over or dropped dead in the street.

'It's been a mighty long time,' said Frankie's mum. 'A lot of water's flowed under the bridge since them days. I'm married now, you know. She told you that, did she? . . . Oh, did she? And what business is it of hers, I'd like to know? What else did she tell you? . . . Oh, really? Did she now? I like her cheek! Just can't resist the temptation to shoot their mouths off, some people. She's even accused me of pilfering the cutlery – me, would you believe!'

The person at the other end didn't seem too interested in Frankie's mum being accused of pilfering cutlery: Frankie's mum didn't refer to it again. The next thing she said, tight lipped, was, 'I don't know about that. I'd have to think about it. You've got no rights, you know – none whatsoever! Any you might have had you forfeited long ago. If I say yes, it's because I'm doing you a favour. And I don't see why I should! Just give me one good reason –'

The conversation went on and on. Frankie couldn't make head nor tail of it. It grew boring after a while, just hearing the one side – it obviously wasn't about Billie Small being run over or dropping dead – so she went back to finish her story.

'Where was I? Where'd I got to?'

Cunningly, Jass said, ''lectwic carving knife.'

'No, I hadn't!' He was trying to trap her. 'I'd got to the bit where the parents caught them and locked them up and gave them sicky pie. And the father kept beating 'em and bashing at 'em till they was all bruises and their brains rattling loose inside their heads.' Frankie still had bruises on her arms from where Billie Small had grabbed her. And her brains still rattled, if she shook her head too hard. They flew round inside and made her dizzy. 'Anyway,' said Frankie, 'one day when the wicked parents was out, something happened. The children heard this loud roaring sound – grrrrraaaaarghrrrfff! – like a tiger, and they went rushing to the window thinking, Oh, it must be a wild animal trying to get through the fence. But it wasn't a wild animal, it was a handsome stranger roaring up in his big powerful motorcar.'

Jass pummelled at his cheeks with clenched fists. 'What kind of motorcar?'

'Big, powerful one.'

'What make was it?'

'American.'

'But what m—'

'Mercedes.'

Jass opened his mouth.

'Cadillac!' Cadillac was American, wasn't it? She looked at Jass. 'All right, then! You choose. The handsome stranger roared up in his –'

'Wolls Woyce.'

'– in his Rolls Royce.'

'White Wolls Woyce.'

'In his white Rolls Royce. And the white Rolls Royce was so powerful and so huge that it crashed straight through the 'lectric fence in one foul swoop to the utter astonishment of all who watched; and out sprang this tall dark handsome stranger, and he came bounding up the fire escape, six steps at a time, so that 'stead of taking him a week to get to the hundred and eighth floor, which was where the children was kept captive, it only took him an hour or two. And down below was the wicked parents, shouting and carrying on something awful. The father was using bad language and the mother was screaming oaths, "I will dig your eyes out, I will knock your block off, I will make minced meat out of you," and both of them shaking their fists as hard as they could as they rushed helter skelter up the fire escape; but however fast they rushed they still could only go one step at a time and soon they was so far behind they began to despair. "We will never catch him!" they moaned. "He will rescue the children and we will have no one left to beat!" So then they had a better idea, they thought they would wait down at the bottom and catch the children as they came out, but what they hadn't realized –'

Frankie paused. From the hall came a click as the telephone receiver was put back.

'What they hadn't wealized –'

'What they hadn't realized,' said Frankie, 'was that the handsome stranger was a whole lot clev'rer than they was, and he disguised the children as something else.'

'What did he disguise them as?'

'Oh –' Frankie waved a hand. Sometimes, right at the end, she grew bored and couldn't be bothered. 'Clowns. Out of a circus. And so they escaped and the wicked parents never saw them again.'

'And they went to live with the man?'

'Yes; they went to live with the man.'

'F'wever an' ever?'

'F'rever an' ever.'

'What does he look like, the man?'

'You know what he looks like!' If she had shown Jass the photograph once, she had shown him a dozen times.

'And he is coming here to wescue us?'

'Yes.'

'When is he coming here to wescue us?'

'Soon,' said Frankie.

'When is—'

'Frankie!' Her mother had come into the room. She crooked a finger. 'Come here! I want a word with you.'

Frankie rolled her eyes. What had she done *now*?

Mutinously, anticipating trouble (it was either the plate she had broken yesterday or the orange juice she had spilt down the back of the sofa) Frankie trailed across the room and followed her mother through to the kitchen. Jass trailed with her. Wherever Frankie went, Jass went too. He was a bit like the pet dog that Frankie had never been allowed to have.

'Well, now,' said her mother. Frankie squared her shoulders. She didn't like it when her mother said, 'Well, now,' in that tone of voice. (It must be the orange juice: the plate had been an old one that had come from the kitchen in Beechcroft Road, but the sofa belonged to Billie Small.) 'Take a seat.' Frankie pulled out a chair and sat down. So did Jass. 'Prepare yourself for a shock.'

The orange juice *and* the plate? Frankie gritted her

teeth: she didn't care! She didn't care if they bashed her and hashed her and—

'That was your father on the telephone.'

He wasn't her father! She wasn't ever going to accept him as her father.

'Your real father.'

'My real father's in J'maica!'

'Not at the moment, he isn't. He's over here on a visit.'

Frankie's eyes spun like Catherine wheels. Her father? Over here? On the telephone?

'It was that Gedge woman put him on to us. I might have known.' Her mother's voice was bitter. 'Stays away for years, doesn't bother to write, never contributes a penny piece, then suddenly turns up, as cool as you please, at the other end of a telephone line, demanding to see his daughter . . . *his daughter!* The cheek of it!'

Frankie's mum flung back her head and gave a rasping kind of cackle. 'What right does he have to call you his daughter? When did he ever trouble himself? I'm the one's had to keep you all these years – I'm the one's had to work her fingers to the bone! That idle good-for-nothing, what's he ever done? Just lazed around in the sunshine, taking life easy, same as he always did. That man never lifted a finger! Not once, in all the time I knew him. And then to have the nerve to come here, making his demands . . . *my daughter,* he says. MY DAUGHTER! Serve him right if I'd said I'd had you adopted – I would have said it, too, if it weren't for that woman! Of course she's already told him, hasn't she? Told him all about the other week's little escapade. I hear *my daughter*, he says, isn't too happy where she is . . . I hear *my daughter* has tried to run away. Well, you can hear this, I says. *Your daughter*, I says—'

'Can I see him?'

'What?'

Frankie pressed forward urgently against the edge of

the table, hands clutching at the sides. 'Can I see him?'

'You can see him if you want. I shan't. I've told him, I'm a married woman now; I've a husband to consider. Belt the living daylights out of me, Billie would. But you can see him. It's all one to me. You go, satisfy your curiosity. I don't doubt you'll come away disappointed. It's not a film star you'll be meeting!'

She didn't want to meet a film star. She wanted to meet her dad.

'He'll have a paunch, I shouldn't wonder. Too much laying around doing nothing. And bald. He'll have lost his hair for sure. That photograph of yours, that was taken a long time ago. He was a young man, then. Ah, we was both young! Young and foolish. I mind well when that photograph was taken, I mind the dress I was wearing. Primrose yellow, it was, with a scooped-out neck and—'

'When?'

'When what?'

'When can I see him?'

'My, you're in a mighty rush all of a sudden! I told him you'd travel up tomorrow. There's to be a cab calling for you at ten, take you to his hotel. In the West End.' Frankie's mum gave a little snort. 'I'd like to know where he gets the money from for *that*. And the cab. He's the one that's going to pay for it – nothing to do with me. He wanted to come and pick you up himself, but I wasn't having any of that. I'll not be having him anywhere near the place. Billie would half kill me, so he would – and I don't blame him! He's my husband; he's a right to be possessive. But you go, if you want. Do you good. I've long suspected you've a feeling the grass might be greener . . . well, you go and find out! You spend the day with him, then you come back here and you tell me. Turning up after all these years –'

Frankie's mum grumbled on: Frankie hardly heard her. Her brain was in a whirl, her head full of thought bubbles, all bobbing up and down in ceaseless motion, like coloured ping-pong balls on a jet of water.

'My dad,' she said to Jass, as soon as they were alone together. 'My dad, come all the way from J'maica. Come to see me. Wants me to spend the day with him. Going to send a cab. Cost a lot of money, cabs do. Cost about – fifty pounds I should think; fifty pounds, easy. You got to be rich, go round in cabs. You ever bin in a cab?'

Jass shook his head.

'Once I done, nearly,' said Frankie, 'when we was in a hurry. Then a bus come and we had to get on that. How about the West End? You ever bin to the West End? I bin to the West End. I bin there when I went on this school trip – see the sights. It's where the rich people go. All them Arabs and things. Hotel in the West End, must cost a bomb. Cost about . . . thousand pounds; least a thousand pounds. Means my dad must have ever such a lot of money. More'n your dad.'

Jass put his thumb in his mouth.

'Well, anyway,' said Frankie, 'I'm going up there to see him.'

She waited for Jass to say something, but he just went on sucking at his thumb.

'You gone dumb or something?' Frankie looked at him, irritably. 'This is my *dad* – man inna photograph! Aren't you int'rested?'

Jass nodded.

'So what's the matter with you?'

Suddenly, she knew what was the matter with him: she was going up to town and Jass was being left behind. Well, and so what? It wasn't his dad! He couldn't expect to go everywhere. 'Can't go *every*where,' said Frankie.

Jass looked at her. His lips quivered as he sucked on his thumb.

'Well, you can't!' said Frankie. It wasn't fair!

Jass turned his head away. Frankie saw a tear go plopping on to the bed.

'Oh, wait there!' she said.

'Take him with you?' Frankie's mum looked at her, suspiciously. She had tended to be suspicious since the escapade over the Heath. 'You're not up to your tricks again, are you?'

'No!'

'So what do you want to take him with you for?'

'Thought he'd like it,' said Frankie. 'Thought it'd make a change for him.' Carelessly, she added, 'Thought it'd make a change for you.'

'Me? I'm not going up there!'

'No, but if I took Jass,' said Frankie, 'you could go and see Olive.'

Her mother was always bemoaning the fact that since coming to Worple Park she never got the chance to see Olive. It wasn't that Olive now lived too far away – in fact she lived nearer to Worple Park than she had to Beechcroft Road – but during the day Frankie's mum was stuck with Jass and Frankie, and in the evenings Billie Small didn't like her to go out. She hadn't seen Olive for ages and ages.

'Well . . . I suppose – oh, very well, then! Take him with you. But your father'll have to pay for him, mind. I'm not giving you the money!'

That was all right, thought Frankie. Her dad wouldn't mind. Her dad was rich.

8

'Don't you forget, now . . . ask him where he's got his money from. Find out what he's been doing. I want a full report!'

The cab had come. The cab driver had knocked at the front door and been sent back down again to wait, because even though Jass and Frankie were ready (they had been ready for the last half hour) Frankie's mum said it didn't do to show yourself too eager. It was vulgar to be eager, it made it look as though you were counting the pennies. Frankie wasn't counting pennies, she just wanted to be off. The quicker she left, the more time she would have to spend with her dad.

'Have you got everything, now?'

'Yes!'

She'd got *every*thing: cardigan in case of rain, clean handkerchief in back pocket, five pound note and name and address safely tucked away in her money belt. (Her mother hated Frankie's money belt. She said a bag would be far more becoming, but Frankie wasn't into bags. Belts were the thing. Belts were macho. Like dungarees: dungarees were macho. Her mother had tried to force her into the little red dress she had worn for the wedding, but Frankie hadn't been having any of that; not when she was going to meet her father.)

'Have you got the money? Have you got your name and—'

'Yes!'

'Well, you just watch it . . . remember what I said.'

What Frankie's mum had said was that the five pound note had come out of her housekeeping and that she wanted it back. It wasn't for spending, but for 'just in case'. The name and address were for just in case, too. Just in case, Frankie supposed, someone should bash her over the head and leave her for dead, so that when she came round and her memory had gone she could look in the purse to find out who she was. ''Cept that anyone bashed me over the head'd probably go and take the purse as well.'

'Who would?' said her mother. 'What are you on about?'

'If I was bashed.'

'Don't talk so daft! No one's going to bash you. It's in case of an accident.'

'Oh.' Frankie explored the idea. 'You mean, in case I fall in the river, or something?'

'Or something.'

'In case the taxi crashes. In case we get hijacked. In case there's a bomb. In case—'

'In case that so-called father of yours walks off and abandons you.' Her mother's lips tightened. 'I wouldn't put it past him. The word *responsibility* simply doesn't enter into his vocabulary. You tell him, I want you home by seven o'clock, no later. Is that understood? Seven o'clock sharp!'

'Can we go now?' said Frankie.

The cab was downstairs, waiting for them. Frankie's mum went round to the driver's door and stuck her head in and said, 'You know we're not the ones that's paying? You know that, do you? It's not up to us.'

'That's right,' said the driver. He jerked his head at Frankie. 'In you get!'

'It'll be no use looking to her. She's got nothing. We d—'

'Lady,' said the driver, 'it's all been taken care of.'

'Well, so long as it has,' said Frankie's mum. She always had to have the last word. She opened the cab door to have yet another. 'You just remember what I told you,' she said to Frankie. 'You keep a hold of that purse – and make sure you're back here by seven o'clock!' As an afterthought she added, 'Have a nice time.'

When the cab reached Trafalgar Square, Frankie knew where they were. Trafalgar Square was where she had come with the school, to feed the pigeons and pose for photographs. It was where the stone lions were, and the fountains. (She and Hake had dared each other to jump in the fountains. They would have done, too, if Kevin Parsons hadn't gone and done it first, and got himself thumped for it.)

The cab went round the Square, up a road which led off it, along another road, up a side street, down another one, and there it was: her dad's hotel. It looked just as splendid as Frankie had always imagined a West End hotel would look, with steps leading up to the doors and a red plastic canopy with fringes and the words 'Mackail's Hotel' written on it in big gold letters. At the bottom of the steps stood a commissionaire in a shiny top hat and a long red coat; and at the top of the steps. . . .

At the top of the steps was Frankie's dad.

He didn't have a paunch. He hadn't gone bald. He was tall and young and slender, just like in her photograph. He was beautiful.

The commissionaire in his red coat and top hat stepped forward to open the door of the cab, but Frankie's dad had already seen them. He was already running down the steps.

'Hi, there!' He held out his arms: Frankie rushed into them. Her dad swung her up, swung her off her feet, hugged her, swung her round. No one in all Frankie's life had ever done that to her before. Not that she could remember. 'So this is my girl! This is my Frankie!'

Frankie's dad held her for a second at arm's length, then, laughing, set her back on the ground. He didn't specially seem to mind that she was a girl. In fact, he didn't seem to mind at all. Maybe over the years he had grown reconciled to it.

'Man, am I glad to see you!' He bunched a fist and cuffed her, playfully, beneath the chin. 'You glad to see me?'

Frankie nodded and beamed till she thought her head would drop off. Her dad . . . her real, own dad!

Frankie's dad suddenly caught sight of Jass, hovering and quivering behind Frankie like a little old palsied gnome. 'What have we here?' He squatted down to look. Jass instantly moved to the other side; so did Frankie's dad. Jass moved back again; so did Frankie's dad. After a few minutes of peep-bo, with Frankie in the middle, being used like a wall, Frankie said, 'Stop it, Jass, and don't be stupid, else I shall wish I hadn't've brought you!'

As a matter of fact she already was wishing she hadn't brought him. If she had known her dad was going to be so gorgeous – he was more gorgeous, even, than Maradona – she wouldn't have done.

'This is Jass,' she said, hoicking him out into full view.

'Hi, there, Jass!'

Frankie's dad held out a hand, but Jass was shy and hid again, clinging to one of Frankie's legs and burying his head in her dungarees.

'He scared of black men?'

'He's scared of everything.'

'How 'bout we try a little coaxing?'

He didn't deserve to be coaxed; showing her up like this! Frankie clenched a fist. 'Look, pack it in, you, or I'll belt you one!'

'Hey! Hey!' Her dad threw up his hands. 'No violence, man! I'm strictly into peace, you know?'

Frankie paused; she looked at him, doubtfully.

'Right on! I mean it. I will run a mile just to avoid the sight of blood.'

She giggled at that. He had to be teasing.

'Just don't try me, okay? I'm not dressed for running . . . not in all this fancy gear.' Frankie's dad was wearing a pair of beautiful white trousers and a peacock blue shirt made out of some shiny, silky sort of material. On Billie Small it would have looked ridiculous. 'Hey! You down there!' Frankie's dad bent and peered again at Jass. 'You hear that? I may be black, but I don't bite . . . it's quite safe to come out. You just take your time. You wait till you good and ready. No rush. We have all day ahead of us.'

In the meanwhile, he said, he and Frankie would go into the tea lounge and eat sticky cakes while they planned the day and decided what they wanted to do. Naturally, if Jass felt brave enough to join them –

Jass couldn't scramble up the steps fast enough. Suddenly, as he reached the top, he came to a halt. He turned, big eyed, clutching at himself. *Now* what was the matter?

'Fwankee—'

Frankie groaned and rolled her eyes. Jass was nothing but a liability; a liability and an embarrassment. She ought never to have brought him. Crossly, to her dad, she said, 'Now he wants to *go*.'

'Go? Already? He only just come!'

Frankie gritted her teeth. 'Go to the toilet.'

'Oh! Is that all?' Her dad grinned as he held open one of the glass entrance doors. 'Don't worry, man – help is at hand!'

While Frankie's dad took Jass off to the gentlemen's toilets (Frankie knew he would rather have gone with her to the ladies', but he was getting too old for that: he'd got to learn *some* time) Frankie was left to sit by herself at a

114

table in the tea lounge and read the menu and look at the cake trolley. She looked so long and so intently – she had never seen so many goodies all stashed together – that a waiter came up and asked her whether she would like to order. She was still ordering as Jass came back with her dad. (Out of the corner of her eye, she noticed that Jass was now holding her dad's hand and talking nineteen to the dozen.)

'I'm ord'ring,' said Frankie. 'That all right?'

'Saves me a job,' said her dad. 'You ordered 'nuff for all of us?'

Frankie hesitated. So far she had ordered one slice of Black Forest gâteau, one slice of strawberry flan, a dish of coffee delight, three cherry tarts and a wodge of lemon meringue pie. Reluctantly, she supposed that it probably would be enough for all of them. Even her imagination didn't quite run to the eating of Black Forest gâteau *and* strawberry flan *and* coffee delight *and* cherry tarts, not to mention the lemon meringue. On the other hand, she wouldn't mind sampling them all. 'I'll just get a bit o' choc'late cake and a—'

'Bag o'chips,' said Jass.

Frankie looked at him, shocked. You couldn't have bags of chips in a tea room! 'You'll have what your given,' said Frankie.

'I want a bag o'chips! I want a—'

'You shut up!' Frankie leaned across and whopped at him with her menu. 'Manners like a *pig*. You can jolly well eat what I've ordered!' Jass opened his mouth. 'I'll tell you what I've ordered, I've ordered Black-Forest-gâteau-an-strawbryflanan-lemonm'ringue'n—'

'Lemon meringue!' Her dad rubbed his hands. 'One of my absolute, all-time favourites, man!'

Jass subsided.

'An' I got three cherry tarts an' all,' said Frankie.

'That,' said Frankie's dad, 'is what I call a good selection. Shouldn't need to eat again for at least half an hour!'

He winked: Jass giggled, happily. Frankie looked at him through narrowed eyes. Something had come over Jass since he had been to the gents' toilet. He had got all bumptious and over confident. She wasn't sure that she approved of it.

Frankie's dad ordered three Pepsis and dismissed the waiter, then leaned back comfortably in his chair. You could tell he was used to posh places, the way he let his legs sprawl out and his arms hang down, just as if he were in his own lounge at home. (Frankie's mum always sat up very stiff and straight whenever she went anywhere. She made Frankie do the same.)

'So what's all this I been hearing 'bout a white Rolls Royce?'

Frankie drew in her breath, sharply. She glared at Jass across the table. He gazed back at her, innocently.

'Tell him, Fwankee! Tell him the story 'bout the wicked pawents.'

She ought never to have brought him. She never would again. Not ever.

'It's only a stupid story,' mumbled Frankie.

'Yeah? I like stupid stories! We tell lots of stupid stories, where I come from. How about you tell me one o' yours?'

'I'll tell!' said Jass. 'I'll tell! 'S all about these childwen what live in this tall big block –'

'*Tower* block.'

'– tow'r block, on the hundwed floors –'

'Hundred and eighth floor!' He might as well get it right.

'– huddad eight floor wiv no lift up down so take people *all day* –'

'All week!' snapped Frankie. 'All week to get up and all day to get down.'

Jass looked hurt. ''S what I was going to say.'

'Well, say it, then! Say it prop'ly.'

In the end, it was Frankie who told the story. She just let Jass tell the last bit, about the Rolls Royce, because that had been his. 'An' they all dwove away in the white Wolls Woyce!'

Frankie's dad said afterwards that it was one of the best stories he'd heard. He specially liked the bits, he said, where the children had to eat all the horrible dishes: 'Scum-an'-matter pie . . . reminds me of school dinner, if I'm not much mistaken!'

'We got annuver one!' boasted Jass. 'We got one where the black pwince come on his horse—'

'Not now,' said Frankie. She had never known Jass burble so much. 'We got cakes to eat!'

'She's right, man! We got cakes to eat.' Frankie's dad dug his fork into one of the slices of Black Forest gâteau and dumped it on Jass's plate. 'You concentrate on getting that inside you.' He pushed his chair away from the table. 'I just remembered something I have to do. Hang on there, I'll be right back.'

Frankie watched as he moved away from them, across the room. She knew a moment of uneasiness. What was it her mother had said? *In case that so-called father of yours walks off and abandons you* . . . She felt, with her hand, for the purse attached to her belt. It was still there, it was all right, she still had her five pound note. But oh, she didn't want him to abandon her! Not now that she had found him again.

'Fwankee –' In his enthusiasm, Jass sprayed gâteau crumbs across the table. 'I like your dad!'

Frankie swallowed. She liked him, too; he was smashing, her dad.

After what seemed an age she saw him coming back to

them, across the tea-room floor, beautiful in his white trousers and silky shirt. She felt ashamed of herself for ever having doubted him. What did her mother know? Her mother was just jealous!

'Look,' she said, 'we saved you some lemon m'ringue.'

After eating his lemon meringue her dad said they must discuss what they wanted to do for the rest of the day. He asked what ideas Jass and Frankie had. Jass, who as a rule never had any ideas about anything whatsoever, and in any case hadn't even been invited in the first place, said that he would like to go to the Tower of London and Madam Two Swords for the waxworks. They were two of the things that Frankie had been going to say. She felt put out, and racked her brains to think of something else. Suddenly, it came to her: 'I'd like to go on a boat on the Serpentine!'

She looked closely at her dad as she said it, but he didn't show any signs of being disturbed by the suggestion. Maybe he had forgotten about going on the Serpentine with Frankie's mum all those years ago when she'd worn her yellow dress. All he said was, 'Okay, that's two to Jass, one to Frankie. Got another one, Frankie?'

Frankie thought of the pier at Clacton, with its slot machines and its helter skelter and the hall of distorting mirrors. 'I'd like to go to a place where you can go on things – switchbacks and things.'

'Sounds like a funfair to me.'

'Yes,' said Frankie, 'a funfair! Let's go to a funfair!'

Frankie's dad took out his *What to do in London* book and after consulting it said they would go to the Tower first, then the waxworks, then the Serpentine, and finally Clapham Common for the funfair. He said that between the waxworks and the Serpentine they would stop off somewhere for lunch, and after the funfair they would stop off for some tea.

'That do you okay? Anything else you can think of?'

Jass said yes, if they had time he would like to go up in a crane, and he would like to look at dinosaurs, and he would like to go to Heathrow and see the aeroplanes, especially Concorde, and he would also like to go to the zoo and feed the elephants and ride on a camel and see the penguins. Frankie, somewhat loftily, said that she thought four places ought to be enough for anyone in one day. 'If they want to do them prop'ly, that is.' She was just trying to work out, to her own satisfaction, which tubes they would have to use (it was a bit difficult since she wasn't quite sure exactly where they were or which the nearest tube station was) when the waiter came back to their table and said, 'Excuse me, sir, your cab is here.'

Cab? Frankie looked at her dad, anxiously. What did he want a cab for? They were going to the Tower! He had said – he had *promised*.

Her dad stood up. 'Ready?' He held out a hand: Frankie latched on to it, fast, before Jass could get there. Jass could jolly well tag on behind! It wasn't his dad.

At the bottom of the hotel steps was a shiny white cab. For them? Frankie stared; so did Jass.

Frankie's dad stepped forward. The commissionaire was standing waiting, cab door held open. 'In you get,' said Frankie's dad.

Frankie felt like royalty. She almost began to wish that she had done what her mother had wanted her to do and worn the red dress.

Frankie's dad got into the cab after them. 'I'm really sorry, man –' he ruffled Jass's hair '– I'm really sorry I couldn't make it a Roller. If I'd've known what was expected of me, well, I would've shifted heaven and earth. But I guess this is better than nothing, huh?'

Jass, wide eyed, wriggled into his place next to Frankie. Two cabs in one day! Frankie tried to be a bit more sophisticated about it. 'You didn't have to bother going to all this expense,' she said. (It was a favourite phrase of her

119

mother's, 'all this expense'.) 'We could've just as easy got the tube.'

'Got the tube? And me a prince? When d'you ever hear of princes gettin' the tube?'

Frankie kicked at Jass. That was his doing, that was; repeating all those silly stories. Just wait till she told her mum. . . .

There were hundreds and thousands of people at the Tower, all babbling away in different languages. The people and the languages were almost more interesting than the Tower itself (though the Jewels were good, and so was Traitors' Gate). Frankie kept looking at her dad in his white trousers and his blue silky shirt and thinking how lucky she was to have someone like that for a dad, someone tall and dark and handsome, rather than some pale pink podgy thing like Billie Small – even though Billie Small was there all the time (more was the pity) and her dad, presumably, was going back to Jamaica.

She asked her dad about Jamaica as they stood queuing to enter the Tower, and he said it was one of the most beautiful places on earth and he wouldn't live anywhere else, 'not for all the Crown Jewels in the world'. He said that Frankie must come on a visit one day. After all, he said, she was his daughter: it wasn't right they should lead totally separate lives. It was time they got to know each other.

'I would've come over before, only until now, you know, man, it's always been a question of bread.' He tapped the back pocket of his trousers. 'Ain't nothing you can do without it. Don't let no one tell you different.'

Frankie remembered what her mother had said as she saw her off from Worple Park. 'Don't you forget, now . . . ask him where he's got his money from. Find out what he's been doing.'

Frankie felt shy about asking her dad where he had got his money from, it didn't seem right. But she could ask him what he had been doing. That wouldn't be rude.

He laughed when Frankie asked him. He said, 'Ridin' the big horses, that's what I bin doin'. Ridin' the big horses . . . It's what you gotta do, you want to get places. Means it's further to fall, of course. You come off, you liable to crack your head, maybe crack it wide, wide open . . . but that's a chance you gotta take.' He stood there, beautiful, in the summer sunshine. 'You can tell your ma, your pa ain't no layabout no more. No, man! He bin ridin' them big horses just as hard as he can. Now he reapin' the benefit. You tell her that. Okay?'

Frankie nodded. She would definitely tell her mother. Riding the big horses . . . her mother would be pleased she had found out.

After the Tower they went to the waxworks. They took another cab, though this time it was just an ordinary black one. (But three cabs in one day – that was really something!)

The waxworks were absolutely brilliant, especially the Chamber of Horrors. The bits Frankie liked best were a man that murdered people in their baths and the guillotine that came swooshing down and chopped heads off. The guillotine was from the French Revolution, which was when the waxworks had been started, by a lady called Madam Two Swords (spelt Tussaud, because of being French).

Frankie could have stayed there in the Chamber of Horrors all morning if it hadn't been for Jass getting scared and starting to grizzle and clutch at trouser legs. He tried clutching at her first, but she shook him off, impatiently – she wanted to go and look at Hitler, and a man being stretched on the rack – so then he went and clutched at her dad, instead, and her dad picked him up and cuddled him, which gave Frankie the same sort of hurt and angry feelings she had had when she had seen Hake going round with Kevin Parsons. He was *her* dad:

Jass had one of his own. When her dad said he was going to take Jass outside, but that Frankie could stay for as long as she liked, she went outside with them, even though it meant missing Hitler and the man on the rack. It wasn't any fun, looking at things by yourself.

After the waxworks they had lunch, sitting at tables laid out on the pavement. Frankie's dad said that it was a carnival day and they could have just whatever they wanted, so Frankie had a pizza and a glass of orange and some tropical fruit salad, and Jass had two helpings of chips and a banana milk shake and a chocolate ice cream, all of which were things that made him sick. (Frankie jolly well hoped he *was* sick. He deserved to be, nasty little glutton.)

From the restaurant they took yet another cab, to Hyde Park and the Serpentine. Jass didn't want to go on the water (probably feeling ill, and serve him right) so he was left on the bank, in the care of the man who hired the boats, and Frankie and her dad went by themselves. Frankie's dad did the rowing: he looked just like he did in Frankie's photograph. Frankie's mum, who had been young when the photograph was taken, had grown up and got old, but Frankie's dad hadn't changed one little bit. He was just as gorgeous now as he had been then, especially when he looked across at her and smiled.

'I took this trip once before, you know.' He closed an eye. 'With another lady.'

'I know,' said Frankie. Greatly daring, she added, 'I've got the photograph.'

'Hey! Is that so? I guess your ma must've give it you.'

'I rescued it,' said Frankie. 'It's in my treasure box.'

'Whaddya know?' Frankie's dad was silent a while, resting on the oars. 'Your ma ever talk about me?'

Frankie dabbled her hands in the water. 'Sometimes.'

122

'What she say?'

'Things.'

'Bad things, I'll be bound!'

'I think she was mad at you,' said Frankie, ''cos of you going away and leaving her.'

'You mad at me?'

Slowly, she shook her head. She had never been mad at him.

'Your ma ever tell you the reason that I left?'

''Cos of me?'

''Cos of *you*?'

'Not being a boy,' mumbled Frankie.

'Hey, man!' Her dad leaned across and gently pummelled her with a clenched fist. 'What give you that crazy idea? I didn't want no boys! Nothing but a load of trouble. Wasn't 'cos of you I left. I just left 'cos we didn't get on. Me an' your ma ... fightin' like cat an' dog we was, towards the end. She wanted for me to get a responsible job, like. Re-spon-sible ... nine-to-five, working for a boss, being pushed around. Man, that just was not me! Not my scene; you know?'

Frankie nodded. It wouldn't be her scene, either. She wasn't going to be pushed around – not by anybody.

'So, I finally did what they was always tellin' us we should – Enoch Powell and all them. I got me a ticket and I went back home; back to ride them big horses. Didn't do it 'cos of all them racists. You don't want to take no notice of them sort. I did it 'cos of your ma. 'Cos I couldn't stand her gettin' at me no more. And man, has it worked out! Best step I ever took, 'cept ... I dunno.' Frankie's dad frowned, and picked up the oars again. 'Mebbe I should've at least kep' in touch. Should at least've written more.'

Frankie brightened. 'I've got a stamp,' she said. 'Once, when you sent a letter ... I got the stamp.'

'I'll send you more stamps. I'll write you. I promise!'
Her dad looked at her, earnestly. 'I'll make up for it.'

Make up for what? Frankie wondered.

The funfair on Clapham Common was called the Great
Original Steam Fair (est. 1885). It had swings and
switchbacks, it had coconut shies and gingerbread stalls,
it had a whirligig whizzer, a ghost rider, a helter-skelter, a
hall of magic mirrors, bumper cars, seesaws, greasy poles,
hooplas, candy floss, toffee apples, and a wonderful old-
fashioned merry-go-round with brightly painted wooden
horses that went up and down, with long flowing manes
and twisty poles for holding on and proper saddles for sitting in. On the inside were the big horses, for adults and
people with long legs: on the outside were the littler ones,
for toddlers and for gnomes. Jass, being a gnome, had one
of the littler ones.

'Fwankee!' He bounced, excitedly, clutching at his pole
and waving at the horse in front of him. Frankie tossed
her head. She wasn't going to ride with toddlers and with
gnomes! Defiantly, she pushed her way to the back and
scrambled on to a big dappledy grey with scarlet saddle,
next to her dad.

Her dad turned, and grinned. 'Livin' dangerously,
huh?'

'Riding the big horses,' said Frankie. 'Like you said.'

He laughed, and stuck up a thumb. 'That's my girl!'

Jass didn't want to get off the merry-go-round. He had
grizzled in the Chamber of Horrors, been too scared (or
too sick) to go on the Serpentine, hidden his head on the
ghost rider, screamed on the whirligig whizzer, sat in her
dad's lap coming down the helter-skelter – and gurgled
with joy as he clung to his pole on the merry-go-round.
Frankie reminded herself that he *was* only seven years old.
It was a pretty small sort of age.

Frankie's dad said that Jass could have another go and

that he and Frankie would wait for him. Frankie wouldn't actually have minded another go herself, but she didn't like to say so; it seemed rather childish. (After all, *she* wasn't seven.) She stood, self important, side by side with her dad, watching as Jass gurgled his way round for a second time. Her dad said, 'Well, I guess he's happy.'

'Mm,' said Frankie.

'You happy?'

'*Mm*,' said Frankie; and she nodded, emphatically, to show just how happy she was.

'You always happy?'

'Well . . . not always.' She thought about it. 'Some of the time I am.'

'How 'bout if you came to live with me? You be happy then, you think?'

Frankie's heart went mad inside her rib cage. Live with her dad? 'In J'maica?'

'In Jamaica, sure!'

'*Could* I?'

'Far as I'm concerned. Course, you'd have to ask your ma.'

'But if *she* said?'

'If she says, then there ain't no problem!'

The taxi stopped at the entrance to the flats. Jass and Frankie got out; Frankie's dad stayed inside.

'I'll call your ma,' said Frankie's dad, 'just as soon as I get back to London. Be about a week – ten days, maybe. I got business to transact. But I'll be back. You tell her.'

'I'll tell her,' said Frankie.

'And don't forget, you ask her – 'bout what we discussed.'

Forget? How could she? It was the very first thing that she was going to do.

9

'So he got you back on time, then!' Frankie's mum must have been lying in wait behind the front door, for she had it open even before Frankie had taken her finger off the buzzer. 'Had enough of you, I don't doubt. Spends one day in the company of his own child and thinks that's his duty done for the next ten years. Have you still got that money I gave you?'

'Yes,' said Frankie. 'Mum—'

'Let's be having it! I'll need that if we're to eat tomorrow.'

'Mum, Dad s—'

'Oh! So it's dad already, is it? First time she's clapped eyes on him since she was in her cradle and she's calling him *dad* already. Doesn't take much for anyone to worm their way into your affections, does it?' She glared at Frankie, as if Frankie had done something wrong.

'Mum,' said Frankie, 'can—'

'Just get yourselves in and sit down! Your supper's on the table.'

Supper? Frankie grew a bit pale. 'It's all right,' she said, 'we've had supper.' After leaving the Great Original Steam Fair they had gone to a hamburger bar and eaten hamburgers and chips and milk shakes, followed by peach melbas. 'Mum, I—'

'What do you mean, you've had supper? Nobody said anything to me about having supper!'

'Dad gave it us. Mu—'

126

'I see! Your dad gave it you. It never occurred to you, did it, to tell him your supper'd be ready and waiting when you got back home?'

'Thought you'd be pleased,' said Frankie. 'Meant you wouldn't have to bother.'

'Well, for your information I already have bothered! I've fixed you one of your favourites – bubble and squeak!'

Frankie swallowed. Bubble and squeak *was* one of her favourites as a rule. But not straight after hamburger and chips and peach melba, not to mention the pizza at lunch time, and the Black Forest gâteau and the strawberry flan and –.

'I suppose he's been filling you up with junk? Rotting your teeth, letting you choose just whatever rubbish takes your fancy! Anything to worm his way in. Well, you're easily bought, that's all I can say! You get in there.' She gave Frankie a little push towards the kitchen. 'You can just sit down and wait while the rest of us eat. I want my supper even if you don't want yours.'

'Mum,' said Frankie.

'Go on! In with you!'

'*Mum*, there's s—'

Frankie stopped. Billie Small was seated at the kitchen table, eating his bubble and squeak.

'What is it?' said her mother. 'What d'you want?'

''S all right.' Frankie plonked herself down on to a chair. Billie Small looked at her, but didn't say anything. He was still mad at her for knocking nails in the wall.

Jass dragged out a chair and heaved it round to Frankie's side of the table. He always sat as close to Frankie as he could.

There was a silence.

'Well, come on, then!' said Frankie's mum. 'You'd better tell us . . . what was he like?'

Frankie pursed her lips. She didn't want to talk about

her dad in front of Billie Small.

'Never tell me he was your dream come true!'

'He was nice,' said Frankie.

'Nice!' Her mother repeated the word, scornfully. 'What she means by that is that he filled them to the brim with junk food and ruined their appetites!'

'We had cakes,' said Jass, 'an' chips.'

'Cakes and chips! I might have known it! Here I go to all this trouble, cooking them a decent meal, and there's he pumping them full of muck!'

Another silence fell. Under cover of the table, Jass sneaked his hand into Frankie's. She let it stay there.

'So what did you do all day? Just eat cake and chips?'

'We went in taxis,' said Jass.

'Went to the Tower,' said Frankie. 'And the waxworks, and –' She was about to say, 'and the Serpentine', but thought better of it just in time. 'And a funfair.'

'Yes, an' I wode onna woundabout!'

'Jass rode on the roundabout.'

'I wode on it two times.'

'And then we had hamburgers.' Frankie looked at her mother, defiantly. Her mother stabbed with a spoon into the middle of the bubble and squeak.

'Oh, he's really been trying, hasn't he? He's really been buying your affections!'

'Pity he didn't buy *them* while he was about it.' Billie Small jerked his head in the direction of Jass and Frankie. 'If he's that keen on 'em, why doesn't he take 'em?'

Frankie opened her mouth – then closed it again. She wasn't going to put her question in front of Billie Small.

'Did you find where he got his money?'

Frankie shook her head.

'Fwankie's dad's a pwince,' said Jass.

'Oh, yeah?' said Billie Small.

Frankie kicked at Jass under the table.

'Black pwince,' said Jass.

Frankie kicked harder. Frankie's mum, spooning bubble and squeak, said, 'Black he may be, but he's no trace of blue blood – not as far as I'm aware.'

'He's having you on,' said Billie Small.

Jass turned, doubtfully, to look at Frankie. 'Fwankee s—'

'I never!' said Frankie.

'The man always was a romancer.' SPLAT went the bubble and squeak, over the side of the pan. 'I never knew such a one for tall tales. Did you ask him what he's been doing with himself all these years?'

'Yes,' said Frankie. She sat up, very straight. 'He's been riding the big horses.'

'Gambling!' There was a note of satisfaction in her mother's voice. 'I might have known it! It had to be one or the other.' She nodded, significantly, at Billie Small. 'Drugs, or gambling, or – you know what.'

'What?' said Frankie.

'Never you mind, miss! I wasn't talking to you.'

'Anyway,' said Frankie, 'he didn't mean gambling.'

'Oh! Did he not? So what do you think he meant?'

'He meant –' Frankie wrinkled her brow, trying to work out just what her dad *had* meant. 'He meant, like –' She knew what he had meant: he had meant that you had to aim high if you wanted to get anywhere. You had to take chances. You had to—

'Gamble,' said Billie Small. 'In a word.' He looked at Frankie, triumphantly.

'He always did enjoy a bit of a flutter,' said Frankie's mum.

'It's obvious: the man's a crook.' Billie Small mopped up the remains of his bubble and squeak and sat back, complacently, in his chair, sawing his right thumbnail up and down between his front teeth, excavating bits of food. 'Probably got half the Jamaican Mafia on his heels.

Probably the very reason he came over here.'

''Tisn't!' said Frankie.

'Go on! Course it is. Plain as day.'

'Don't kid yourself,' said her mother, 'that he came just to see *you*.'

Frankie reddened: she had thought that, just at first. 'He's got business to tr –' She paused, trying to remember the word. 'To translate.'

'Oh, yeah?' said Billie Small. 'Oh, yeah?' He spat a piece of food, which he had just succeeded in dislodging from his teeth. 'That's a good one! Believe anything, some people.'

She hated Billie Small. She *hated* him.

It wasn't till later in the evening, when Billie Small had gone to the pub and Jass been sent to bed, that Frankie had the chance to ask her question. 'Mum,' she said, 'c'n I go to J'maica?'

'Go to Jamaica?' Her mother stared. 'You must be joking! Where would I ever get the money for you to go to Jamaica?'

'Go there with Dad . . . to live. You wouldn't have to find any money, he'd pay.'

If her dad could afford to stay in West End hotels and travel everywhere in cabs, he could surely afford to pay for Frankie to go to Jamaica? He wouldn't have suggested it, otherwise.

'If you think,' said Frankie's mum, 'that your precious father would want you over there, living with him—'

'He asked me!' said Frankie. 'He said!'

'What did he say?'

'He said that if you said it was all right, then I could go.'

'To live with him?'

'Yes! Can I? *Please*? Can I?'

'He was pulling your leg.'

'He wasn't,' said Frankie. 'Honest! He's going to telephone you.'

'When?'

'When he gets back from –' Frankie hesitated. 'From doing his business.'

Her mother gave a short laugh. 'I'll believe it when it happens!'

It would happen; Frankie knew it would. Her dad had said that he would telephone, and he *would* telephone, like he had said that he would send a cab and he had sent a cab. 'Can I go?' she said. '*Can* I?'

'What for?'

''Cos I'd like to!'

'Why?'

''Cos he's my dad!'

'And what am I? No one, I suppose!' Her mother leaned forward and began angrily punching buttons on the television set. 'Oh, you go if you want! Don't mind me . . . I'm only your mother! I'm only the person that gave birth to you and looked after you and cared for you all these years. My feelings aren't important, they don't matter, you do what you want to do; I'm surprised you even bothered consulting me!'

Frankie looked at her mother, uncertainly. 'He said I'd got to ask you first.'

'Did he now? That's most thoughtful of him! What am I supposed to do, go down on my knees and say thank you? Thank you very kindly . . . I've only the one child, take her by all means! What do I care?'

There was a pause. Loud noises came from the television set. Hectic pictures filled the screen. (Jass must have been playing with the colour controls: all the faces were lobster red.)

'You could always have more children,' said Frankie, 'now that you're married.'

'More? What would I want with more? One's bad

131

enough! For all the gratitude one gets.'

'I wouldn't go away for ever,' said Frankie. She couldn't imagine going away for *ever*. 'I'd come back and see you.'

'Oh! Would you? That's mighty nice of you.'

'I'd come back . . . every holidays.'

Frankie's mum gave a short laugh.

'I would,' said Frankie. 'Every holidays. And we'd go to Clacton and go onna pier.'

'Would we now?'

Frankie could tell that her mother didn't believe her. She didn't believe that Frankie would come back. She really thought she wanted to go away for ever and ever. Suddenly, Frankie had an idea: 'You could come with us!' Her mum, her dad, and Frankie . . . she was sure her dad wouldn't mind. 'We could all go together!'

'I've no intention of going to Jamaica! Or anywhere else, if it comes to that. I've a home, and a good man. I know when I'm well off. What would I want to go to Jamaica for? No, thank you! You go if you want. What you do is up to you. But you needn't think I'm sacrificing everything I've lived and worked for just to up and keep you company. Oh, dear, no! You go, you go by yourself. But just remember one thing . . . you'll have made your own bed, it'll be up to you to lie on it.'

Frankie was silent a moment, pondering the possible meaning of this remark. It didn't really seem to have one. What had beds to do with it? She was talking about *Jamaica*. After a bit, anxiously, in case there had been some mistake, she said, 'Does that mean, when he rings, I can say yes?'

'I said so, didn't I? What more do you want?'

She wanted to be able to say yes right now. She wanted to be *certain*. She wanted to pack her bags and be waiting, ready to go. She wanted to know when she could go. She wanted to talk about Jamaica. She wanted to talk about what it would be like and where she would live, whether it would be in a house or a flat, whether there would be sea, whether she could go before school started, whether schools in Jamaica would be the same as schools in England, whether she would have to have a passport, how long it would take to get one, whether they would go by air, and if so would it be Concorde, and –

'Why don't you get off to bed?' said her mother. 'It's way past your bedtime.'

Experimentally, in the bedroom, Frankie said: 'I'm going to go to J'maica and live with my dad!'

Jass didn't hear her, because he was asleep.

She thought about Jass as she lay in bed, counting sheep and listening to next door's television. She remembered that other time when she had lain and counted sheep – no, when Jass had counted them; in their hidey hole on the Heath, when they had tried to run away. Jass wouldn't like her going to Jamaica. He would cry.

Well, and so what? What was she supposed to do about it? This was her dad, not his! He'd already got a dad; he'd had one for seven whole years. And anyway it would do him good. Teach him to stand on his own feet. He couldn't drag round after Frankie for the rest of his life.

He would be able to have a bedroom all to himself. He would like that.

No, he wouldn't: he would hate it. He would be frightened. He would start wetting the bed again, and Billie Small would start walloping him. Jass hadn't had an accident in the bed for nearly three weeks, now. He'd even stopped sleeping with the light on.

Well, too bad! *Too bad*. Frankie pummelled crossly at her pillow. She jolly well wasn't going to stay here just for Jass.

* * *

Next morning, ages and ages before she was ready to open her eyes, she felt her cheek being dabbed at and heard Jass's voice, impatient, in her ear: '*Way*kup, Fwankee! Fwankee, *way*kup!'

Grudgingly, Frankie prised open an eyelid. She looked blearily at Jass from her one eye. 'Whozzmadder?'

'We going see your dad again today?'

'No.' Frankie let her eyelid fall back.

'When we going see him 'gain?'

She didn't know that Jass ever was going to see him again.

'Fwankee?' He dabbed at her. 'When we going see your dad?'

'Some time.'

'Your dad's a nice dad. I like your dad.' Jass curled up, confidingly, next to Frankie. 'When will he come an' wes-cue us?'

Frankie frowned. 'That was just a story. Like in a book. Doesn't mean it's going to happen.' It *was* going to happen, of course, to Frankie. Not to Jass.

Jass was crinkling his nose. Frankie could tell he was struggling to make sense of what she had said. 'Fwa—'

'Get up!' said Frankie. She gave him a shove. 'Time to get up!'

Her mother was in a mood and wouldn't speak to her. Frankie's mum got like that sometimes. She'd got like it once when Frankie had told her how Mr Harding said she was like his granddaughter, and she'd got like it another time when Frankie had asked if she could go and live with the lady in the sweetshop. She said to Jass, 'Your break-fast's on the table. Get and eat it then go off out. I don't need you under my feet this morning, I've work to do.' She didn't say anything to Frankie; just yanked the vacuum cleaner from the cupboard and went clanking off with it.

'Got her knickers in a twist,' said Frankie.

Jass, looking scared, as he always did when anyone was angry, sank on to a chair and began shaking out cornflakes. Frankie tossed her head. She wasn't scared! She picked up a piece of leathery toast, smeared it with jam and went off after her mother.

'Mum!' She had to bellow over the noise of the vacuum cleaner to make herself heard.

'What?'

'Want to ask you something!'

'I'm surprised you've got the nerve.' Her mother switched off the vacuum and stood, arms folded, looking down at her. 'Well? What is it?'

'C'n Jass come to J'maica with me?'

'Oh, no! No, no! No way! You're not taking him. If you go, you go by yourself!'

'B—'

'I said no!'

'But he said, yesterday! He said!'

'Who said?'

'*Him – Billie.*'

'Said what?'

'Said it was a pity Dad didn't buy us.'

'Buy you!' Her mother gave one of her laughs; short and sarcastic. 'An offer would be a fine thing!'

Frankie wasn't sure what that meant. Did it mean that if her dad *did* make an offer – ?

'Will you stop scattering toast crumbs all over? As if I don't have enough to do!'

The vacuum cleaner resumed its deafening roar. Frankie leaned over the back of the sofa to scream. 'I don't see what you want to keep him for. All you ever do is bash him!'

Her mother turned, in a fury. 'How dare you, Frankie Foster? I've never bashed that boy yet!'

'*He* does! He does it all the time!'

'That's his right, he's his father! And that's why he's not

135

going off to Jamaica with you! Some parents,' shouted Frankie's mum, 'like to feel their children have a bit of natural affection for them!'

Frankie and Jass spent the morning in the park. Jass begged for stories, but Frankie didn't feel like it. She didn't feel like anything very much. She could have gone and climbed the wall, had a look over to see if Queenie and Mrs Thatcher were there – what did she care for Billie Small, now that she was going to Jamaica? – but she couldn't seem to summon up the energy. Even thoughts of beautiful Guy weren't enough to tempt her.

'Look!' said Jass. He tugged her hand. 'There's them boys.'

'What boys?'

'Them ones what you fighted.'

Frankie, without much interest, raised her head. (She had been studying a woodlouse, curled into a ball. Woodlice weren't particularly inspiring, but then she wasn't feeling inspired.)

'Where?' said Frankie.

'There!' Jass pointed. Down a path at right angles to them strutted Ginger Top and Batman. Batman was wearing a T-shirt which said 'I gotta lotta bottle'. Ginger still had teeth marks halfway up his arm. Frankie looked at them, contemptuously. 'Ignore them,' she said. 'Just keep walking.'

Jass gulped and clutched her hand. He would have liked to run, but she wouldn't let him; running would be fatal.

'They can't do nothing to you,' said Frankie. 'Not s'long as I'm here.'

Jass trembled slightly, but he didn't whine or grizzle or try to pull in the opposite direction as once he would have done. He trusted Frankie: he felt safe when he was with her.

The two paths were on a direct collision course. Any second now –

'Watch it, wog!' Ginger hissed the words venomously in Frankie's ear. 'I got plans for you!'

Frankie marched on, eyes fixed, looking neither left nor right. Ginger's voice pursued her down the path: 'Got plans for him an' all!'

Frankie's hand closed hard over Jass's. 'Take no notice. They can't do nothing.'

'How'd you feel if your little brother was to disappear one day? How'd you feel if he was cut up and fed to the sharks? How'd you—'

'Drop dead,' said Frankie.

'And you!' yelled Ginger. 'You'll be sorry, Nog Face! You just wait! You'll be sorry!'

Frankie spun round. 'You touch him and I'll burn out both your eyes with a laser beam!'

'Yeah?'

'Yeah!'

They stood, glaring at each other. Batman heaved a kick at Ginger's left foot. 'Let's go! We got better things to do than stand here all day.'

'Yeah.' Ginger nodded. 'That's right . . . we got better things to do.'

'So why not go and do 'em, then? Sick head!'

Ginger took a step forward. Batman hauled him back.

'You just watch it,' said Ginger. 'You just watch it!'

Honour satisfied, Ginger allowed himself to be dragged away. Frankie, with a loud scoffing noise, turned on her heel. It was a long time before Jass said anything; and when he did, in a small voice, all he could manage was: 'Fwankee—'

''S all right,' said Frankie. 'They're not gonna get you.'

'But Fw—'

'It's all *right*,' said Frankie. 'I told you!'

Back at home, Frankie's mum was still in a mood. (They usually lasted at least twenty-four hours.) 'You can get your own lunch,' she said. 'I haven't the time, I've things to do.'

It wasn't easy, getting lunch. Frankie's mum had decided that one of the things she had to do was clean out the kitchen, which meant buckets of soapy water standing in the middle of the floor and a pair of steps propped in front of the fridge, not to mention all the kitchen chairs piled on top of the table and the draining board full of crockery, cups and plates stacked like the Leaning Tower of Pisa halfway to the ceiling.

'We'll have ravioli and bread 'n butter,' said Frankie. She said it loudly, so that her mother could hear. If her mother didn't want them to have ravioli, then she could say so. Frankie's mum didn't say anything, she just picked up one of her buckets of water and noisily clattered the steps across the floor.

'I'll open the tin,' said Frankie, 'you c'n get the plates.'

Of course she should never have asked Jass to get the plates; she realized that afterwards. He wasn't tall enough to reach the top of the pile: it probably seemed quite logical to him to take them from the middle. There was a terrible crash as they all tumbled down. Bits of plate shot all over the kitchen. Frankie's mum screeched and slapped her bucket on the floor.

'You clumsy little so and so!' She aimed a blow, catching Jass a sharp clip under the chin. 'Of all the stupid things to do! What's the matter with you?' She seized Jass by the shoulders and shook him. His head wobbled on the end of his neck like the head of a rag doll. 'Are you completely mindless? Don't you have any brain? I begin to think your father was right! He always said you were a moronic little twerp! You're worse than that, you're like some kind of cretin! You wet the bed, you—'

'Leave him alone!' shouted Frankie. She hurled herself at her mother, pulling at her, tearing at her clothes. 'It's not his fault, he can't help it! They're only stupid plates!'

'You shut your racket if you don't want a thick ear!'

'Then stop going on at him! All the time, going on at him!'

'I'll go on at him if I want to go on at him! I'll do what I like in my own home! What's it to you? You don't belong here any more, you're getting out – and the sooner the better as far as I'm concerned! Good riddance, that's what I say! You can go and pack your bags right now.' Her mother had stopped shaking Jass. She stood, hands on hips, glaring defiance at Frankie. 'Well? Go on! What's stopping you?'

Frankie tried not to look at Jass, cowering by the sink. She knew that his eyes would be on her, huge and saucerlike.

'Did you hear what I said? I said—'

'I'm not going.'

Her mother cupped a hand round her ear. 'You're what?'

'I said, "I'm not going!" '

'Oh! So you've changed your mind, have you? And what's brought that about? Got cold feet? Had second thoughts? I knew you wouldn't do it when it came to the point! You're no fool, are you? Too well aware which side your bread's buttered. Well, all I can s—'

'SHUT UP!' Frankie turned and ran from the kitchen, racing for the shelter of her bedroom and slamming the door behind her. 'I hate you!' she sobbed. 'I hate you, I hate you, I hate you!'

'There now, Frankie love! Don't take on so!' Frankie's mum knelt by the side of the bed as Frankie sobbed angrily into the pillow. 'You'd never have liked it in a foreign country anyway. You'll do much better staying here where you belong. I'll make it up to you, I promise.'

She reached out a hand and stroked Frankie's hair. 'Things'll be better from now on. We'll all be a family, doing things together and having fun and – all the things that families do. There'll be Christmas, and birthdays and – ah, come on now! Dry those tears and give us a smile. We're going up the road, all three of us. There's the *Jungle Book* on. I said I'd take you, didn't I? The next time it was here? Well, now it is, so let's be going. I'll show you! Your dad's not the only one knows how to have a good time . . . you'll see!'

Because Frankie had missed lunch she was allowed to have two ice creams and a bag of popcorn to eat in the cinema; and afterwards, on the way home, they stopped off at the local supermarket to buy something for supper and Frankie was the one who got to choose. (She chose crinkle-cut chips and crispy cod fries followed by strawberry flan with jelly and real cream.) As an extra special treat her mother said she could have the latest single by the Lead Pistons, who were Frankie's favourite group and who she usually wasn't allowed to listen to (on account of grown-ups thinking them repulsive). She was even allowed, for the first time in weeks, to watch 'Pop Box' on the television, despite Billie Small being there and grumbling because he wanted the cricket.

It was like having a birthday. It would have been silly not to make the most of it. She played the new single five times in a row – her mother said, 'Lord, Frankie! You really like to get your pound of flesh, don't you?' – and kept Billie Small waiting till the very last credit had rolled on to the screen, the very last note of Pop Box had died away, before she let him turn to his cricket. But, in the end, she still had to go to bed.

She had thought that Jass was asleep. She had been sure

that he was asleep. She had crept past him on tiptoe and he had never even stirred. She jumped when the gnome-like shape in its blue spotty pyjamas appeared by the side of her bed. 'Fwankee?'

'What?' She spoke with her face half muffled in the pillow.

Jass put his cheek close to hers. 'Evewything's be all wight, Fwankee.'

Stupid idiotic gnome! What did he know?

'Fwankee?' Jass stretched out a finger and poked experimentally at her eye. 'You cwying, Fwankee?'

Frankie scrubbed her nose along the bottom sheet. 'Course I'm not!' What would she be crying for? In one movement, she flipped over on to her back. 'Want me to tell you a story?'

Jass nodded, ecstatically. 'Tell a stowy!'

When Jass had settled at the end of the bed, she began: 'Once upon a time, there were two children. The children were called –'

'Jass an' Fwankee!'

'Jass and Frankie. They lived in a tower block, on the h–'

'Huddad an eight floor!'

'– hundred and eighth floor. And there weren't no lifts –'

'No liffs!'

'– which meant you had to walk all the way up and all the way down, and sometimes –'

'– people died!'

'Sometimes people dropped dead, 'cos of not having brought enough food. That was on the way up. On the way *down* . . .'

It was a long story; even longer than usual. It was so long that after the first few minutes Jass gave up telling Frankie what people's names were and what happened next and lay curled in a heap, with his thumb in his mouth, listening.

'. . . and just as the parents was about to catch up with them, what d'you suppose happened? This big silver bird swooped down out the sky and – are you listening?' said Frankie.

Jass made a mumbling sound.

'You're not to go to sleep, otherwise I shall stop.' She prodded at him. 'Listen! This big silver bird swooped down, and it was as big as – as an armchair! And the children jumped on to it in the nick of time, because just as it rose into the air the wicked parents arrived, but too late to do anything. They could only stand there helpless, shaking their fists and yelling, "You come back here you ungrateful horrid children!" But all to no avail: the children had gone. And even though they sent aeroplanes after them the aeroplanes couldn't catch up because the bird was a magic bird that flew one million times faster than the speed of light and it took them to this place where the black prince was waiting. It was him that had sent the magic bird to rescue them. The magic bird was his. And so was the place where he was. The place was his kingdom where he ruled. It was the most beautiful place on the whole of the earth. It was always sunny and–' Frankie broke off. 'You're asleep!' she said.

He was! The horrible nasty little gnome! He had actually gone to sleep on her. Frankie wrenched indignantly at her pillow. Some people just didn't *deserve* getting rescued.

Jass, deprived of his share of pillow, stirred and mumbled. 'Fwa—'

'Shuddup!' Frankie pushed his head back down. 'Go to sleep!'

Stupid *gnome*.

BEAVER BOOKS FOR OLDER READERS

There are loads of exciting books for older readers in Beaver. They are available in bookshops or they can be ordered directly from us. Just complete the form below and send the right amount of money and the books will be sent to you at home.

☐ THE RUNAWAYS	Ruth Thomas	£1.99
☐ COMPANIONS ON THE ROAD	Tanith Lee	£1.99
☐ THE GOOSEBERRY	Joan Lingard	£1.95
☐ IN THE GRIP OF WINTER	Colin Dann	£2.50
☐ THE TEMPEST TWINS Books 1 – 6	John Harvey	£1.99
☐ YOUR FRIEND, REBECCA	Linda Hoy	£1.99
☐ THE TIME OF THE GHOST	Diana Wynne Jones	£1.95
☐ WATER LANE	Tom Aitken	£1.95
☐ ALANNA	Tamora Pierce	£2.50
☐ REDWALL	Brian Jacques	£2.95
☐ BUT JASPER CAME INSTEAD	Christine Nostlinger	£1.95
☐ A BOTTLED CHERRY ANGEL	Jean Ure	£1.99
☐ A HAWK IN SILVER	Mary Gentle	£1.99
☐ WHITE FANG	Jack London	£1.95
☐ FANGS OF THE WEREWOLF	John Halkin	£1.95

If you would like to order books, please send this form, and the money due to:
ARROW BOOKS, BOOKSERVICE BY POST, PO BOX 29, DOUGLAS, ISLE OF MAN, BRITISH ISLES. Please enclose a cheque or postal order made out to Arrow Books Ltd for the amount due including 22p per book for postage and packing both for orders within the UK and for overseas orders.

NAME ....

ADDRESS ....

....

Please print clearly.

Whilst every effort is made to keep prices low it is sometimes necessary to increase cover prices at short notice. Arrow Books reserve the right to show new retail prices on covers which may differ from those previously advertised in the text or elsewhere.